Vasilisa the Wise

& Other Tales of Brave Young Women

Retold by KATE FORSYTH
Illustrated by LORENA CARRINGTON

A DIVISION OF EDC PUBLISHING

First American Edition 2019
Kane Miller, A Division of EDC Publishing

Text copyright © Kate Forsyth 2017
Illustrations copyright © Lorena Carrington 2017
First published in Australia by Serenity Press Pty Ltd, 2017

Library of Congress Control Number: 2018942399

Manufactured by Regent Publishing Services, Hong Kong
Printed November 2018 in ShenZhen, Guangdong, China
1 2 3 4 5 6 7 8 9 10

Paperback ISBN: 978-1-61067-852-0
Hardcover ISBN: 978-1-61067-979-4

For my own wise brave girl, Ella. K.F.

For Mari & Rosa, who have always known which dragons to slay, and which to befriend. L.C.

Contents

Foreword

I have loved fairy tales all my life.

I love their eerie beauty and perilous darkness, and their dreamlike landscape in which it seems all things are possible.

Fairy tales were the earliest stories told by our ancestors, invented to enchant and entertain on one level, and to teach and warn on the other.

For fairy tales have two faces, one open and one hidden. On a conscious level, they are stories of true love and triumph and transformation, bringing reassurance that good can overcome evil, love can prevail over hatred, and darkness shall be banished and light returned to the world.

They also work on a much deeper subconscious level. Speaking in symbol, motif, metaphor and archetype, they express and exorcise our deepest psychological fears and desires, and help shape our sense of ourselves and the world.

For many young women, though, the only fairy tales they know are the ones that have been retold by Walt Disney Studios. Singing teapots, dancing mice and heroines with wasp-thin waists and sweet voices abound.

And if they have encountered other fairy tales apart from the Disney collection, they are almost certainly stories that had been told by men. Charles Perrault. The Brothers Grimm. Hans Christian Andersen. The result has been that many wonderful old tales have been drained of their feminine power.

Once upon a time, these stories of magical transformation were meant for young women as they grew away from childhood and towards adulthood. They were told by their mothers and grandmothers and the wise women of the clan as they spun and wove and stirred their pots and made their potions. The heroines of these old tales set out on a difficult road of trials to discover their true destiny. And, contrary to popular opinion, marrying a prince was not the only goal. These ancient tales of wonder and adventure are about learning to be strong, brave, kind and true-hearted, and trusting in yourself to change the world for the better.

I have long wanted to bring back some of the old stories that have been lost to us, stories that celebrate feminine strength and wisdom, and which subvert some of the stereotypical ideas of what women can and should do. I wanted to give my own daughter stories that taught her that girls could be just as clever and fearless as boys, and had just as much right to be the agent of their own lives.

One day I bought the most beautiful piece of fairy tale art from an Australian photographic artist, Lorena Carrington. I wrote to her to express my love for her work, and we began to correspond. We discovered that we were both interested in these old tales of female empowerment and wanted to bring them back to life. We began to work together, exchanging stories and ideas and images. Slowly Lorena and I made this book together. We knew we wanted to write a book for young women, just setting out on their life's adventures, and we knew we wanted the stories and the artwork to be full of darkness and peril and tension, just as the old stories always were. It was a journey of discovery for both of us, and for our daughters who modeled for many of Lorena's exquisite photographs.

When it was time, we reached out to see if anyone would want to publish our work and found – through the most wonderful workings of chance – the perfect publisher in Monique Mulligan of Serenity Press in Australia. The three of us have worked together, like the three spinners of destiny, to bring you this book of forgotten tales about brave young women stepping from the shadows and back into the light.

We would like all of you who read this book to remember that you carry within you the power to change your world. No matter how hurt or afraid or silenced you feel, you can find deep within you the strength to stand up and speak out, fighting against the witches and ogres of your world, just like Vasilisa the Wise and Katie Crackernuts and their sisters.

Kate Forsyth, 2017

"Vasilisa the Wise" is a Russian variant of the Cinderella tale in which a young and beautiful girl is mistreated by her stepmother and stepsisters, and is sent by them to the fearsome Baba-Yaga to fetch fire. She outwits the old witch and ends up marrying the Tsar. It is an old oral tale first collected by Alexander Nikolayevich Afanasyev between 1855-67 and published in *Russian Fairy Tales*.

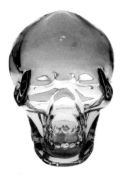

Vasilisa the Wise

Long, long ago, in a Tsardom far away beyond high white mountains and vast icy steppes, there lived a merchant and his wife. They had only one child, a daughter named Vasilisa, and the three of them lived together in great peace and contentment. One day the merchant's wife fell ill. She called her daughter to her.

"My dearest child, I am dying." With difficulty, she sat up and pulled out a tiny wooden doll that she pressed into Vasilisa's hands. "With my blessing, I leave to you this doll, which my mother once left to me. Carry it with you always and never show it to anyone. When evil threatens you or sorrow befalls you, take it from your pocket and give it something to eat and drink. You may then tell it your trouble, and it will help you." She kissed her little daughter on the forehead. Shortly afterwards, she died.

Vasilisa grieved greatly for her mother. Her sorrow was so deep that when night came, she lay in her bed and wept and did not sleep. Eventually she remembered the wooden doll. She rose and went to the kitchen, where she tore off a fragment of bread and poured out a thimbleful of milk and set it before the doll.

"I am so sad, little doll. Can you help me?" she whispered.

The doll's eyes began to shine like fireflies, and suddenly it became alive. It ate a morsel of the bread and took a sip of the milk, while Vasilisa told her all her woes.

"Do not sorrow and do not weep, but close your eyes and go to sleep. For morning is wiser than evening," the little doll said.

Vasilisa lay down, the doll in her arms, and the next day her tears were less bitter.

So it went on for a long time, with the doll comforting Vasilisa and giving her the strength to go on.

The merchant grieved for many months too, but the time came when he thought it best to marry again. His eye fell on a widow with two daughters of her own. They would be company for his little Vasilisa, he thought, and so he married the widow and brought her home as his wife.

Now Vasilisa's stepmother was a cold, cruel woman, who had married the merchant for the sake of his wealth. She had no love for Vasilisa. All day she screeched about the house:

> "Come, Vasilisa! Where are you, Vasilisa?
> Fetch the wood, don't be slow!
> Start a fire, mix the dough!
> Wash the plates, milk the cow!
> Scrub the floor, hurry now!"

Her own daughters lolled about, curling their hair and painting their toenails, while Vasilisa's fingers were worked to the bone. She had the help and comfort of her mother's little wooden doll, however, and so she was able to endure. Each night, when everyone else was sound asleep, she would creep from her bed and find scraps of food for the doll.

"I am so lonely, little doll. Will you talk to me?" she would say.

The doll's eyes would shine like glowworms. It would comfort her and tell her stories of the past. And while Vasilisa slept, the doll would prepare all the work for the next day, so Vasilisa did not have to toil so hard.

One day the merchant had to travel to a distant Tsardom. He bade farewell to his wife and her two daughters, and kissed Vasilisa goodbye. She watched him ride away with an awful sinking in her stomach, fearing what her stepmother would do.

That night the merchant's wife called the three girls to her and gave them each a task. Then she

went about the house, secretly dousing every fire and candle till it was so dark the girls could not see.

"It is now too dark to work," the stepmother said. "One of you must go to Baba-Yaga's house to ask for a light."

Vasilisa shrank back. Baba-Yaga was a witch who gobbled up people the way wolves devoured rabbits.

"I'm not going," said the eldest daughter. "I am making lace, and my needle is bright enough for me to see by."

"I'm not going," said the second daughter. "I am knitting stockings, and my needles are bright enough for me to see by."

But Vasilisa was spinning flax, and she could not see a thing.

Her stepmother laughed and said: "Vasilisa must go! Get yourself to Baba-Yaga's house this minute, Vasilisa, and ask her for a light." And she pushed Vasilisa out the door and locked it behind her.

Vasilisa shivered with fear. The blackness of night was about her, and the rustling and murmuring of the forest, and the wild cold wind. She took out her little doll, and drew a crust of bread from her pocket to feed it.

"O dear little doll, I must go to Baba-Yaga for a light, but I'm afraid she'll eat me with one great bite. Whatever shall I do?"

The doll's eyes began to shine like two stars and it became alive. It ate the crumbs and said: "Do not fear, Vasilisa, my dear. No harm shall come while I am here."

The light from the doll's eyes beamed out through the darkness, revealing a narrow, crooked, winding path through the forest. Holding the doll close, Vasilisa started out on her journey.

The forest was tangled with thorns and hung with gray moss. Vasilisa stumbled along the path, following the light from the doll's eyes. When she heard hooves galloping behind her, she leapt out of the way. A man crouched on the back of a horse raced past. He was arrayed in white, and his horse was white as milk, and the harness was silver. As he passed by, the darkness lifted and birds began to sing. Vasilisa's steps quickened.

For long hours she hurried along, and then another horse galloped past. The rider was robed in red, and his horse was red as blood, and the harness was scarlet. As he passed her, the sun rose high into the sky.

Vasilisa was hungry and tired and footsore, but she pressed on, following the path deep

12

into the forest. The shadows lengthened, and the sky dimmed. Then a third man on horseback came galloping up. He was clad in black, and his horse was black as coals, and the harness was made of iron. As he passed her, the sun set and the forest was plunged into darkness. Vasilisa clutched her doll closer, and kept on following the narrow path.

A long time later, she saw lights ahead of her. In a clearing among the trees, a wretched hut stood on skinny chicken legs, surrounded by a fence made of bones and crowned with skulls. All the eyes of the skulls were lit up and were gleaming red.

The house began to dance about on its chicken legs, jumping up and down as if in anticipation. The trees groaned, the branches creaked, and the wind howled. Dry leaves whirled up and spun around Vasilisa, who shrank back in fear.

A huge iron mortar skidded along the path. In it was crouched an old woman, her arms and legs as thin as toothpicks, her filthy gray hair whipping behind her. In one hand she held a pestle, which she used to propel the iron tub forward. In her other hand was a kitchen broom made of silver birch twigs, which she used to sweep away her tracks. Her teeth were iron, sharpened to points.

Sniffing all around her, Baba-Yaga cried:

"I smell flesh and blood so sweet,
who is here for me to eat?"

Tucking her doll safely away, Vasilisa stepped forward. Her knees were trembling. "It is only me, Vasilisa. My stepmother sent me to you to borrow some fire."

"Did she? How very kind of her," the old witch said. "Well, I give nothing away for free. You must work hard to earn your fee. If you fail, I'll guzzle you for tea." Baba-Yaga shrieked with laughter, then cried: "Unlock, my bolts so strong! Open up, my gate so wide!"

The gate of bones swung open, shrieking as if the motion caused it pain. Baba-Yaga flew in. Vasilisa crept behind her, but a birch tree by the gate lashed Vasilisa with its frail, dry branches. "Do not whip the maid, birch tree. It was I who brought her here," said Baba-Yaga.

A thin, mangy dog snapped at Vasilisa.

"Do not bite the maid, dog. It was I who brought her here," the witch said.

Then a bony cat lashed out at Vasilisa with its sharp claws.

"Do not scratch the maid, cat. It was I who brought her here."

Baba-Yaga smiled at Vasilisa, showing her pointed iron teeth. "You see, you will not be able to escape easily from here, Vasilisa. My cat will scratch you, my dog will bite you, my birch tree will lash you, and my gate will bar your way."

Vasilisa tried not to show her fear. *At least I am not alone*, she told herself, putting her hand inside her pocket to touch the little wooden doll.

All the while, the witch's hut kept spinning around on its skinny chicken legs, shrieking and creaking.

Baba-Yaga struck the ground with her pestle and cried, "Hut, hut, turn your back to the forest and your front to me."

Slowly, the hut stopped spinning, and came to rest facing them. Its door screeched open, and a rickety ladder slid out. The witch flew in, but Vasilisa struggled up the ladder. It was much bigger inside than seemed possible from the small size of the hut. A huge black stove with a red fiery mouth dominated one wall, while dozens of legs of ham and plucked birds hung with ropes of onions and garlic from hooks in the ceiling.

"I'm hungry," Baba-Yaga said. "Feed me well, or I shall decide to eat you instead."

So Vasilisa hurried to find the old witch something to eat. She brought her a pot of beetroot soup and a loaf of bread, but Baba-Yaga was still hungry. She brought her a haunch of ham and fried up six dozen eggs, but Baba-Yaga was still not satisfied. So Vasilisa cooked up twenty chickens, forty geese and sixty doves, which the old witch devoured in just a few bites.

"I'm thirsty," Baba-Yaga shrieked. Vasilisa brought her beer by the barrel and milk by the pail. Soon nothing was left but a heel of dark bread and a dribble of milk. Vasilisa ate and drank eagerly, but made sure to keep a little back for her doll.

Baba-Yaga glared at her with bloodshot eyes.

"Now, Vasilisa," said she, "while I have my nap, you must take this sack of millet and pick it over seed by seed. And mind that you take out all the bad ones, for if you don't, I shall eat you up."

And Baba-Yaga stretched out on her enormous iron stove, closed her eyes and began to snore.

When she was sure the witch was asleep, Vasilisa took the thin crust of bread, and the few drops of milk, and offered it to her doll.

"I am so afraid, little doll. The task she has set me is impossible. Can you help me?"

The eyes of the doll began to shine like two candles. "Do not sorrow and do not weep,

14

but close your eyes and go to sleep. For morning is wiser than evening."

Vasilisa did not think she could possibly sleep, but she was exhausted from her long journey. She curled up on the floor, shut her eyes and soon her breathing relaxed.

The doll called out:

"Birds of the air, hear me,
There is work to do, you see.
Come in answer to my call,
You are needed, one and all."

Flocks and flocks of birds came flying, more than eye could see or tongue could tell. They began to sort the seeds, the good into one sack and the bad into another. And before they knew it the night was gone and all the work done.

When Vasilisa awoke and saw the sacks of sorted seeds, she thanked the birds and promised to never forget to put out food for them, then hugged her doll tightly.

"Beware, Vasilisa, keep your wits alive, if this day you are to survive." And the little wooden doll crept wearily into Vasilisa's pocket again.

When Baba-Yaga woke, she was amazed and angry to find the task had been done. Scowling and growling and stamping about, she told Vasilisa to scrub the house from top to bottom, and milk the cows, and peel a great pile of muddy potatoes. "I'm off to hunt. Mind, now, if you do not do it all, I shall eat you up."

Vasilisa nodded and watched as the witch jumped into her iron mortar. Just then, the man in red galloped out on his blood-red horse, and the sun rose high into the sky.

"Who are the horsemen?" Vasilisa dared to ask, remembering them from the forest.

Baba-Yaga grinned, showing her iron teeth. "They are my Bright Dawn, my Red Sun and my Black Midnight."

"Where do they ride?" Vasilisa asked.

"They hunt each other across the sky."

"But why?"

Baba-Yaga looked at Vasilisa, and her grin grew wider and wider, so that her iron teeth glittered.

"Never mind," Vasilisa said, holding up both hands and backing away.

Baba-Yaga laughed. "She is wise for one so young. And now I hunt!" She brought down her pestle, and with a spray of sparks the mortar launched into the sky, the old witch hunched inside, sweeping away her tracks.

Vasilisa fed the cat and the dog, whose bones showed sharp under their skins, and watered the birch tree's parched roots. Then she fed her little doll and begged it for help. And the doll called out in ringing tones:

"Come to me, mice of house and field,
There are pots to scrub and potatoes to peel!
Come in answer to my call,
You are needed, one and all."

And the mice came running, swarms and swarms of them, more than eye could see or tongue could tell, and before the day was over the work was all done.

Night fell as the black horseman galloped past the gate. The eyes of the skulls crowning the fence glowed red. The trees groaned and the wind howled, and Baba-Yaga came riding home, sweeping behind her with a broom.

She was furious when she saw how everything gleamed, and the great pile of peeled vegetables. She stamped about and mumbled and grumbled, and after she had eaten an even bigger dinner than the night before, she went to bed.

The third day passed in much the same way as the first, though this time it was the ants that came to Vasilisa's help. Baba-Yaga was angrier than ever, and when she went to bed Vasilisa heard her mutter:

"Crack her bones and suck them dry,
Roast her flesh and boil her eyes,
Mash her brains and make mince pies,
Tomorrow that girl shall surely die!"

Once again Vasilisa put some milk and bread before her doll, and watched it come to life, its eyes glowing like tiny suns.

"You must escape," the doll told her.

"But how? Will the cat not scratch me, the dog bite me, the birch tree lash me, and the gate bar my way?"

"Think what you may do for the cat and the dog and the tree and the gate, then they will think what they can do for you."

Vasilisa thought hard. Then she hugged her doll and put it into her pocket, and crept through the house, finding what she needed. She gave the cat a bowl of cream, and the dog a thick slice of red beef. She watered the birch and cleared away the weeds choking its roots. Then she took some oil and greased the hinges of the gate of bone. The gate swung open for her, and she ran through. Only the red glowing eyes of the skulls saw her pass.

Seeing them, Vasilisa thought, *I can't go home without any fire or my stepmother will be angry.* So she lifted down one of the skulls and used it to light her way through the forest. By the time the white horseman galloped past she was far away.

Baba-Yaga woke and, seeing that Vasilisa was gone, bounded to her feet.

"Did you scratch Vasilisa as she ran past?" she asked the cat.

"No, I let her pass, for she gave me a bowl of cream," the cat replied. "I served you for many years, Baba-Yaga, but you never gave me so much as a drop."

Baba-Yaga rushed into the yard. "Did you bite Vasilisa as she ran past?" she asked the dog.

"No, I let her pass, for she gave me meat to eat. I served you for many years, Baba-Yaga, but you never gave me so much as a bone."

"Birch tree, birch tree!" Baba-Yaga roared. "Did you lash Vasilisa?"

"No, I let her pass, for she watered my roots and cleared them of weeds. In all the years I have been growing here, you never gave me a single drink."

Baba-Yaga ran to the gate. "Gate, gate!" she cried. "Did you lock her in?"

"No, I let her pass, for she greased my hinges. I served you for ever so long, but you never cared how I shrieked."

Baba-Yaga flew into a temper. She tried to break the gate but it flew back and knocked her down. She shook the birch tree but it lashed her with its branches. She beat the dog, but it bit her. She kicked the cat, but it scratched her. Tired and sore and bruised, she shook her fist at the forest and shouted, "Good riddance to you, Vasilisa. I'm better off without you." And then she greased the gate's hinges, watered the birch tree, threw the dog a bone and fed the cat

some milk, and settled down to enjoy her dinner.

Meanwhile, Vasilisa ran through the forest till she had almost reached her home. Her steps slowed when she saw there was still no light on in the house. Her stepmother and stepsisters had been looking out for her, and now rushed out and began to chide and scold her.

"Stupid girl! What took you so long fetching the fire?" her stepmother demanded. "We have tried to strike a light again and again but to no avail. We have been so cold and hungry and afraid. Perhaps your flame will keep burning."

And the stepmother stepped forward and tried to seize the skull. But its blazing eyes fixed themselves on her and her two daughters and burned them like fire. The stepmother and her daughters screamed and tried to hide but, run where they would, the eyes followed them and never let them out of their sight till all three were burned to cinders.

Vasilisa screamed with horror, but the burning eyes of the skull did not harm her. With shaking hands, she took out the little doll, and fed it a few crumbs and a thimbleful of milk. "Little doll, little doll, the fire I brought from Baba-Yaga has burned my stepmother and sisters to ashes. What should I do?"

"Bless them and bury them," the little doll said. "For they wanted you dead, but you are alive."

So Vasilisa gathered up the skull and the ashes, and buried them in the garden, saying a blessing in a shaking voice.

"Now, Vasilisa my dear, do not weep, but close your eyes and go to sleep. For morning is wiser than evening," the doll said.

The weary Vasilisa slept with the doll in her arms all night. In the morning, she found a great bower of red roses growing where she had buried the skull and ashes.

Vasilisa's father soon came home. He was sorry to hear of the danger she had been in, but grateful that she had survived, with the help of her doll and her own quick wits. As for Vasilisa, she was overjoyed to have her father home safe again.

The years passed, and Vasilisa grew up, but the little wooden doll was never far from her. It was always glad to be fed a little bread and milk, and come to life and talk to her. In time, Vasilisa won the heart and the hand of the Tsar himself, and became known as Vasilisa the Wise for her goodness and kindness and cleverness.

But that is another story, to be told another time.

Kate says:

I have drawn on the version "Vasilisa the Beautiful," translated from the Russian by Irina Zheleznova and published in 1966 by Progress Publishers. I have always loved the tale for its brave heroine Vasilisa and for the terrifying Baba-Yaga, one of the most interesting characters in world folklore.

Chosen by Lorena, who says:

The Baba-Yaga stories are some of my favorites. While Baba-Yaga's strength is in her wild and ferocious power, Vasilisa's strength comes from her kindness, and the "blessing," in the form of her doll, of maternal wisdom. This contrast and clash between them makes for a compelling read. Baba-Yaga herself was fantastic fun to illustrate. I created her from sticks and leaves: the detritus of the forest floor. My Baba-Yaga is a woman of the wilderness. She is part of the forest, she protects it, and also commands over it. Her world is not ours, as our world is not for her, and I think that's what makes her so fearsome.

"Katie Crackernuts" tells the story of how a brave and clever girl sets out to save her sister from dark magic, and ends up saving a young lord as well. It is an oral tale collected by Andrew Lang in the Orkneys in 1889.

Katie Crackernuts

In Scotland, a long time ago, there lived an earl with a beautiful daughter whose name was Lady Kate. She was sad and lonely, for her mother had died when she was a baby. So the earl decided to marry a woman who had a daughter just the same age as his. Her name was also Kate. She was not at all beautiful, but was so kind and clever and merry hearted that the earl's daughter loved her like a sister. The two girls – one golden haired and bonny, the other dark haired and bright – shared everything, though the elder was called Lady Kate and the younger was simply Katie.

The new countess was a proud and jealous woman, with lips as thin as a line drawn in red. It angered her that Lady Kate was so much more beautiful than her own daughter. It seemed to her that Katie was always cast in the shade. What chance would Katie have of winning herself a rich and noble husband when her stepsister drew everyone's eyes away?

One day the countess heard of an old cunning-woman who lived in the forest and knew all sorts of spells and charms and curses. She wrapped herself in a hooded cloak and went to the cunning-woman, and offered her a bag of silver pennies if she would put some kind of bane upon Lady Kate and mar her beauty forever.

The cunning-woman was old and bent as a tree blown sideways by the wind, her eyes as sharp as pins. She chuckled as she tucked away the bag of coins. "I have just the hex for that. Send her to me tomorrow, but make sure she does not break her fast."

The next morning the countess sent Lady Kate to the forest to collect some eggs from the cunning-woman. "Be quick about it, my dear, and you shall have the brownest egg for your own," she said.

Lady Kate did as she was told, but was so hungry that she caught up a heel of bread from the kitchen on her way out and gobbled it down as she went. She found the cunning-woman's cottage, in a dark and shadowy grove, all overgrown with briars and poisonous weeds: baneberry and bloodroot, deadly nightshade and hemlock, stinging nettles and wolfsbane. Her heart quailed, but she went and knocked on the door and asked for eggs, as she had been told to do.

The cunning-woman pointed to a huge iron cauldron boiling away on the fire. "Lift up the lid, my lassie, and you will see them."

Lady Kate peered into the cauldron, but saw nothing but a thin soup bubbling away. "I cannot see any eggs," she said.

"Go home and tell the countess she needs to keep her larder door better locked," said the cunning-woman crossly.

Puzzled, Lady Kate went home and gave her stepmother the message. When she saw how angry the countess was, she grew a little afraid, though she could not think what was wrong.

The next morning, the countess sent Lady Kate to collect the eggs again but this time she accompanied her to the castle's front gate, to be sure her stepdaughter did not break her fast. Kate was hungry, though, and so she ate some berries from the hedgerow along her way. Inside the tumbledown cottage, the cunning-woman was waiting for her with eyes as sharp as needles. Once again Lady Kate was told to look inside the bubbling cauldron, but once again she saw nothing but soup.

The old woman said angrily: "Tell the countess that the pot won't boil if the fire's away."

So Lady Kate went home and, trembling and faltering, told her stepmother what the cunning-woman had said.

The next day, the countess told Lady Kate that she would walk to the cunning-woman's house with her, to make sure she did the job right. Lady Kate did not want to go, but she could not disobey her stepmother and so together they walked to the forest. Every time Lady Kate reached for a berry or a wild apple, her stepmother would slap her hand and mock her for being too plump, and so the poor girl went hungry.

The cunning-woman was waiting for them in her cottage, her ragged shawl wrapped tight about her, her eyes as sharp as a steel trap. Again Lady Kate was commanded to lift the lid off the pot, and so – troubled and afraid – she did as she was told. This time, however, she saw a sheep's head bobbing about in the boiling soup.

Crying out in alarm, Lady Kate jumped back but the sheep's head bounced right out of the pot and landed on her head. No matter how she pulled at the sheep's head, she could not get it off, and all her cries sounded like a sheep bleating.

In horror, Lady Kate ran out of the cottage. Behind her, she heard the cunning-woman and the countess laughing, and the clink of coins being exchanged. Bleating piteously, Lady Kate hurried home, hiding behind trees and hedges as she went so no one would see her.

Back in her room, Lady Kate stared at herself in the mirror. From the neck down, she was as bonny as ever, but from the neck up she was as woolly as a winter sheep, with a long snout, golden eyes, and twitching ears. "Baaaa!" she sobbed. "Baaaaa!"

That was how her sister Katie found her.

"What has happened? Who did this to you?" Katie flung her arms about the poor girl with the sheep's head, kissing her soft woolly snout tenderly.

"Maaaaaa," Lady Kate bleated. "Maaaaaaa."

Katie understood that it was her own mother who had done such a terrible thing to her sister. She thought long and hard about what to do, and then she wrapped a fine silk shawl about Kate's head, took her by the hand, and they both went out into the world to seek their fortune.

The two girls walked and walked, and at last came to another castle, which grew on the verges of an immense forest. Katie knocked at the door and asked the housekeeper for a night's lodging for herself and her sister, her face all muffled up in a shawl.

"We don't want any more sickness here," the housekeeper said. "The earl's eldest son is sorely ill, and we're all at our wit's end to know what to do for him."

"Perhaps I can help," Katie said. "I'm used to looking after my sister."

"I couldn't be asking you to help our young lord," the housekeeper said. "Anyone who sits the night with him disappears, and now no one dares stay with him."

"I will sit with him," Katie said, "if you will give us a quiet room where my sister can rest and be at peace."

So the housekeeper agreed, and led them to a small room with two beds where they could rest, and brought them up some supper. Poor Lady Kate found it very hard to eat, but Katie cut the food up for her very fine and so the poor exhausted girl was able to swallow it down and then retire to her bed. However, Katie was still full of energy. She went to the kitchen and said, "I am ready now to sit with the sick lord."

"You are very brave," the housekeeper said. "Do be careful. A dozen servants have all been sent to watch over him, and all were never seen again."

Katie was a little afraid but also very curious. Besides, she had to find some way to support her beloved sister. She was taken to meet the earl and his younger son. They too looked wan and worried, and warned her about the dangers.

"We do not know what happened to all that sat with him before," the earl said. "We've searched high and low, and near and far, but not a single sighting of them have we found."

"I do hope you can help him," the younger brother added. "We're afraid he will soon die if we cannot find the cure for him."

"I'll do my best," Katie promised them.

She was taken to the young lord's bedchamber, and shown how to bathe his fevered brow with lavender-scented water and give him cool teas made of lemon balm and willow bark. He was a comely young man, with dark sweat-damp curls and hollow cheeks, but he was sunk in a restless sleep. As midnight approached, his dreams became more agitated. He threw off his blanket and tried to get up. "Help me," he sobbed. "Please help me."

"I'll do my best," Katie promised again, and he quieted at the sound of her soft, sweet voice.

As the midnight hour sounded, however, the sick lord jumped up, pulled on his fine velvet doublet and his boots, and went downstairs. Although Katie called to him and tried to hold him back, he simply shook her off and went on his way. The lord went to the stable, called his hound, saddled his horse, and then mounted. Katie leapt lightly up behind him as he kicked his horse into a gallop.

On and on, they rode through the shadowy greenwood. Katie began to fear they would never stop. They came to a green hillock set in a glade of nine hazel trees. Katie reached up

and plucked a handful of hazelnuts, for she was hungry. The lord dismounted, and Katie thrust the hazelnuts into her pocket and slid down to the ground behind him.

The lord caught up a hazel branch from the ground and rapped it upon the side of the hill. "Open, open, green hill, and let the lord in," he cried.

Katie quickly added, "And his lady behind him."

The green hill split open and showed a long hall that reached deep into the earth. At the far end of the hall was a vast ballroom, blazing with light. Music rang out, and dancers spun past the doorway. The lord hurried down the hallway, leaving his horse and hound in the moonlit glade. Katie slipped after him, keeping to the shadows, as the hill closed behind them.

As soon as the lord entered the ballroom, many beautiful young faery maidens swooped upon him, leading him into a whirling, twirling, swirling dance. They were dressed in the most extraordinary gowns, made of leaves and flowers and feathers and iridescent beetle wings. Their hair flowed down their backs, pinned with knots of ribbons and red haws. Their feet were bare. Dancing with them were tall elves with fine-boned faces, squat dwarves with beards to their knees, grinning goblins with green-hued skin, and tiny fluttering things that shone with a silvery light.

At the far end of the hall, a tall pale woman sat upon a carved wooden throne, her hands clenched. She wore a gown of dark-green yew needles and a crown of poisonous red yew berries upon her writhing black hair. The music was wild and free and strange, played on instruments carved from bone and hung with teeth. The lord danced and danced and danced. Every time he tried to stop and rest, he was dragged once more to the floor.

The more he danced, the more pale and dizzy he grew. Katie's heart was struck with pity. But she dared not show her face, for she saw that the servants who toiled in the shadows were all human. They were thin and bowed down with grief and exhaustion. Many still wore the ragged livery of the castle beside the forest. Katie guessed they were the servants who had followed the sick lord and had been caught by those of faery kind. Katie resolved not be caught too.

The lord danced on. Sweat rolled down his face and he staggered as he spun. The faery maidens dragged him on with ruthless hands and jeering faces, while the queen with the yew-berry crown watched with burning eyes.

"Twirl him, whirl him, hurl him!" she cried.

"We shall teach his father not to defy me! Refuse to pay the faery tithe, does he? Well, we shall take our payment in the life force of his eldest son."

At last the cock crowed. The lord stumbled from the ballroom, pushed and shoved by mocking hands, his eyes as dazed as if he was sleepwalking. Katie crept behind him, keeping to the shadows.

"Open, open, green hill, and let the lord out," he cried.

"And his lady behind him," Katie whispered.

The green hill opened and let them out. Katie helped the lord onto his horse, and held him steady as they rode home in the chill gray dawn. He slid down from his horse, and left it still saddled, head hanging. He was so weary he could scarcely put one foot before the other. Katie helped him into his own bed, and then she soothed him to sleep with a lullaby. When the earl and his younger son came anxiously to see him, they found Katie sewing by the fire and the lord sleeping peacefully.

"How did you do it?" the earl demanded, but Katie only smiled and offered him some hazelnuts.

"Will you sit by him again tonight?" the earl asked.

"For a bag of gold crowns," Katie said. The earl agreed at once.

The second night happened as it had before. The lord rose at midnight, and rode his horse through the moonlit forest, not noticing Katie clinging close behind him. He danced and danced and danced, till his body swayed with exhaustion, but still the faeries urged him on, never allowing him any rest. And all the while the faery queen watched, eyes hot with hate in her bloodless face.

Katie could not bear it. If the young lord was forced to keep on dancing like this, night after night after night, he would surely die. She had to find some way to rescue him. Greatly daring, she crept from pillar to pillar until she was crouched at the very foot of the queen's great throne. It was in Katie's mind to seize the queen, and hold her hostage till she released the spell she had lain upon the young lord. It was a mad, wild plan, born of desperation. If she failed, Katie knew she would be trapped in the underground kingdom forever.

Katie wished she had a weapon of some kind. Looking around her, she saw a faery child playing on the floor nearby. He had a wand made from a hazel twig in his hand. With three quick strokes, he turned a lizard into a tiny winged dragon, spitting sparks and plumes of smoke. As the dragon launched itself into the air, the faery child touched it again, three times, in quick succession, and the dragon was transformed into a dragonfly, whirring its transparent wings.

"If only that wand was mine," one mortal servant grumbled to another. "We could change ourselves into giants and smash our way free of this accursed place."

Katie's heart leapt with hope. She thought for a while, then put a hand in her pocket and drew out some hazelnuts. Taking off her shoe, she cracked a nut open with one quick, hard thwack! The faery child looked up. Katie smiled, and offered him the sweet nut in its broken shell. He crawled close enough to take it from her hand and ate it greedily. He held out his hand for another and Katie shook her head. She showed him the cluster of nuts in her hand and then gestured towards the hazel wand. He frowned, and Katie shrugged and put the nuts back in her pocket. In less time than it took to draw a breath, the faery child pushed the wand into her hand and begged for her hazelnuts. Katie smiled, took the wand, and gave him the nuts. Her heart sang. Surely, with the wand's help, she would be able to save the poor exhausted young man, dancing till his feet were bruised and bloodied?

The cock crowed. The young lord stumbled towards the gateway to the ordinary world. "Open, open, green hill, and let the lord out," he cried.

"And his lady behind him," Katie whispered once more.

The green hill opened. The lord staggered into the gray of early morning, too weary to mount his horse by himself. Katie heaved him into the saddle, then jumped up and took the reins. With the young lord slumped against her back, she rode his horse home.

As soon as she could, Katie rushed to her sister's room and saw her lying asleep in bed, her sheep's head resting on the pillow. "Wake up, Kate, wake up," she cried.

Her sister yawned and sat up and stretched. Katie struck her lightly three times on the head, wishing with all her heart to see her sister's bonny face again. To her great joy and relief, the sheep's head dissolved away, and there was Lady Kate, smiling at her. The sisters embraced.

"Thank you, sweet Katie," Lady Kate said. "Does this mean we can go home again?"

Katie shook her head. "The poor lord is still sick, and all his faithful retainers are slaves under the hill. I must save them."

Her sister nodded. "I will get up then and go and see what I can do to help in the castle."

Katie went to tend the young lord. The earl sat by his son's bed, his shoulders hunched. He looked up as she came in and said, "Do you dare stay another night? For he sleeps more peacefully with you here."

Katie looked into the earl's tired, kind face, and said,

"If I stay, if I save him from this spell, will you let us marry? For, indeed, I love him truly."

The earl smiled at her and said, "If my son so wishes, I'll be glad to have you as my daughter."

He looked to his second son for his opinion, but the young man was gazing out the window, watching golden-haired Lady Kate as she sang, cutting herbs and flowers in the garden. Katie smiled.

The third night passed as the first and second had done. The lord rose at midnight and rode away to the green hill and the faery ball. Katie went with him, gathering a handful of nuts as they rode through the hazel grove. The lord danced and danced and danced. This time Katie did not watch, but looked for the faery child. He was crouched behind the queen's throne, teasing a little bluebird in a cage.

The lord danced past, almost falling as he spun, and one faery maiden turned and whispered behind her hand to another: "If only he knew that three bites of that wee birdie would make the sick lord as well as ever he was."

Katie's pulse quickened. She could scarcely breathe with hope and joy. She cracked hazelnuts for the faery child until he at last consented to trade the bluebird with her. He opened the cage and then – with a wicked grin – wrung the bird's neck, so that it fell down limp and dead. Katie was sorry for the poor little thing, but she hid the bird under her apron, knowing it was the only way to save the young lord.

As the cock crowed and the lord turned to limp home, Katie slipped the hazel wand to one of the captured servants. "Three taps of the wand and magic will happen," she whispered.

Light-footed, Katie ran after the lord and helped him to mount and ride home, supporting him in her arms. He was so weak and worn out, he could barely take a step without her. She got him safe into his bed and built up the fire. Then Katie plucked the bird and cooked it upon the fire.

A delicious smell filled the room. The sick lord roused and lifted himself onto one elbow. "Oh, I wish I had a bite of that birdie."

Katie gave him a slice of the roast bird, and he ate it with great relish. Color crept into his cheeks. He raised himself up higher. "Oh, if I could just have another bite of that birdie!"

Katie gave him another slice. He sat up on his bed, his hair tousled, eyes bright. He looked at Katie as if seeing her for the first time. "May I have more?"

So Katie gave him a third slice, and he ate it hungrily, smiling at her. "Will you not join me?" he asked.

Blushing, Katie ate a little. It made her happy to see him sitting up so strong and well, eating and talking and laughing. When the bird was all gone, he made a sad face and said, "But I'm still hungry."

Smiling, Katie drew out a bushel of hazelnuts from her pocket.

As she cracked them for him, she told him about all their adventures until a great commotion roused them. Running to the window, they saw a ragged crowd of the earl's servants marching home, grinning and waving, and Katie knew they had broken free of the faery knoll. She and the young lord ran hand in hand to the great hall, where they found Lady Kate, hand in hand with his younger brother.

So, the sick brother married the well sister, and the well brother married the sick sister. And all were bright and bonny and hale and hearty from that day forth, and never again troubled by the faery folk under the hill.

Chosen by Kate, who says:

"Katie Crackernuts" was collected by Andrew Lang in the Orkney Islands and published in Longman's Magazine in 1889. In the original tale, both girls are named Kate. Joseph Jacobs edited and republished the tale in his *English Fairy Tales* (1890), but changed the elder stepsister's name to Anne to avoid confusion. I, however, like the two sisters having the same name (perhaps because it is mine), and so have gone back to the original oral version.

The story reminds me of the Grimm tale "Twelve Dancing Princesses," but I like this one much better as the girl rescues her sister and the lord. In the original tale, no mention is ever made of all the servants who vanished, so I had my Katie rescue them as well. I first read this tale in the novel *Kate Crackernuts* written by Katharine Mary Briggs which I bought in a second-hand bookstore in Scotland – it has been a favorite of mine ever since.

Lorena says:

I love "Katie Crackernuts" for its focus on female friendship and solidarity: a rare theme in fairy tales, especially between stepsisters. While Katie rescues the lord because she has grown to love him, her motivation was not romantic love, but love for her stepsister.

The image of poor Lady Kate running home with her new sheep head was one of the simplest illustrations to assemble. The silhouetted figure is created from just two photographs. However, that photograph of the sheep was one of the most difficult to get. Did you know that sheep are incredibly camera shy?

"A Bride For Me Before a Bride for You" is the tale of a young woman who marries and then outwits a giant serpent in order to save her childhood friend. A 19th century Norwegian fairy tale, it was first included in *East of the Sun & West of the Moon: Old Tales from the Norse,* edited by Peter Christen Asbjørnsen and Jørgen Engebretsen Moe, and translated into English in 1859.

A Bride For Me
Before a Bride For You

Once upon a time, there lived a fine young king who was married to the most beautiful of queens. They were very much in love and happy as could be. However, as the years passed and the queen failed to bear any children, their happiness turned slowly to sadness.

One day the queen walked in the forest by herself, so her husband would not see how wretched she was. She came to a shadowed pool beside a thorn tree, and sat beside it. As her tears fell, they dropped one by one into the water, and sent out ever-widening ripples across the gleaming dark water.

An old woman, bent and hunched over a gnarled staff of thorn, hobbled out of the shadows. "Why so sad, my pretty lady?"

"It's no use my telling you," answered the queen, "nobody in the world can help me." And her tears flowed more quickly, though she tried to hide them.

"One never knows," said the old woman. "Tell me your trouble, and maybe I can help."

"I long for a child of my own," the queen said, crumpling her handkerchief in her hand, "but my husband and I have not been so blessed."

"Do not weep," the old woman said. "I can help you with that." She fumbled in the sack upon her back and drew out a small silver cup. It had two handles, like a child might use. "Fill this cup with water from this tarn under the thorn tree. Carry it home without spilling a drop, then – at the very moment the sun sets – pour the water onto the ground in a hidden part of your garden, where no one can see. Place the cup upside down on the damp soil."

She gazed at the queen with intense, dark eyes. "When the sun rises in the morning, lift up the cup. You will find two roses underneath it: one red and one white. If you eat the red rose, a little boy will be born to you. If you eat the white rose, a little girl will be your blessing.

"But, whatever you do, you mustn't eat *both* roses,
or you'll be sorry, that I warn you!
Only one. Remember that!"

"Thank you, a thousand times." The queen took the cup eagerly. "This is good news indeed!"

She offered a gold ring in payment, but the kind old woman would not take it. "I have no need of gold. The forest gives me all I need." Leaning heavily on her staff, she limped into the trees and vanished from sight.

The queen filled the silver cup with water from the thorn-shadowed pool, and walked slowly back to the castle, careful not to spill a single drop. She poured out the water at sunset, and turned the cup upside down upon the damp soil. Excitedly, she went to bed, unable to wait for the morning. At first light, she was awake, ready to lift up the little drinking cup.

Underneath grew a little rosebush, on which blossomed two roses. One was red, the other was white. The queen gazed at the flowers in joy and amazement. Their sweet perfume filled the air, dazing her senses. She bent to smell one, and then the other, unsure which rose to choose.

If I eat the red rose, she thought, *and I have a little boy, he may grow up and go to the wars and be killed. But if I choose the white rose and have a little girl, she will stay at home awhile with us, but later she will marry and leave us. So, whichever I choose, I may be left with no child after all.*

She clasped her hands together, unable to decide. At last she put out one trembling hand, plucked the white rose and ate it. So sweet it tasted that she forgot the old woman's solemn warning and ate the red rose too.

Months passed, and the king left to fight in the wars. While he was away, the time came for

the queen to give birth. It was late, and she was all alone in her bedroom. The birth pangs were cruelly sharp but blessedly brief. Eagerly, the queen bent to see her child. To her horror, it was no newborn babe that she had birthed, but a serpent, green as poison, cold as a tomb. The queen screamed when she saw it and flung it away from her. The serpent slid away into the shadows. Nobody seemed to have seen the serpent but herself. The queen tried to slow her racing heartbeat.

It was just a nightmare, she told herself. *Those red glaring eyes I see are just coals in the fire. That hissing I hear is just the flames devouring the wood.*

But she had no time to think of the serpent anymore. Another child demanded to be brought into the world. At last a little boy was born, pink as dawn, warm as life. The queen was radiant with joy. So too was the king when he returned, and found his son and heir.

No one knew that the queen had given birth to a serpent. It was as if it had never existed. The queen thought about it now and then, with a shudder, but told herself it had all been an awful dream.

Yet, as the years passed, word came that some dread creature preyed upon the outlying villages, killing livestock and destroying the harvest. A giant serpent, people whispered. Green as poison, cold as the tomb.

The queen felt chilled to her core. But she dared not confide in her husband, for fear of what he would say.

Her son grew into a handsome young prince. Bright and merry, he was happiest out in the gardens and the woods, playing with the gardener's daughter Flora, or riding with his horse and hounds. The king and queen doted on him and gave him all he desired, but he was always quick to share his toys or help those in need.

One day, the prince met the daughter of a neighboring lord at a castle ball. She was lovely as spring, as gentle as a turtledove. The prince fell in love with her at first sight. "Papa, Mama, I have met my one true love," he declared. "I wish to spend the rest of my life with her. Have I your permission to court her?"

Overjoyed, the king and queen gave him permission to visit her and press his suit. The prince set off in the royal coach, drawn by six white horses. But his way was blocked at the very first crossroads by the coils of a great serpent, green as poison, cold as the tomb.

"A bride for me before a bride for you!" it cried, its forked tongue flickering.

The prince shouted to the coachman to turn the coach around and gallop away. The horses reared and bolted, the whites of their eyes flashing in their terror. The coachman tried to find a different route, but it was no use. At the next crossways, the serpent lay heaped in heavy green coils. "A bride for me before a bride for you!" it demanded again.

Again the prince ordered the coach to turn, again they tried to find another road, again the giant serpent blocked the way, demanding a bride for himself.

So the prince had to turn back and return home to the castle, unable to declare his love for the young lady, unable to ask her to marry him. He was cast into misery, and the royal court was in turmoil, wondering what it all meant. The queen had to confess that she had – long ago – given birth to the serpent.

"Please forgive me for not telling you earlier," she said, wringing her hands. "I thought it was just a dream … a terrible dream."

"How strange," the king said. "How awful. That serpent … that dreadful creature … is our son?"

"And our firstborn," the queen answered, wiping away tears. "By rights, he should be married first."

"That … that snake … is my brother?" the prince asked in a tone of disbelief. "And the true heir to the throne?"

"So it would seem," the king replied heavily.

The prince grinned. "Well, that's a relief. For I never really felt I was made of the right sort of stuff to be king. Well, I suppose we shall just have to find the poor old fellow a bride of his own. Get him married off, and then I can go and woo my one true love like I want to."

So the king wrote to all his neighboring kings, but none were willing to sacrifice their daughters to such a terrible beast. It seemed as if their younger son would have to stay unmarried. Worst of all, the serpent prince spent the days and nights sliding through the streets of the town about the castle, causing chaos and terror everywhere he went. Every time the young prince tried to ride out to hunt or visit friends, the serpent lay in wait, flickering his forked tongue and demanding: "A bride for me before a bride for you!"

"I'd find one for you if I could," the prince cried. "But nobody wants to marry a serpent, I'm afraid."

The serpent hissed in the most terrible way. The prince backed away, hands held high, then ran to find his father.

"You must find a bride for my brother!" he cried.

"I don't know where I am to find her," his father replied. "I have already made enemies of many great kings by asking them to send their daughters here!"

It seemed as if nothing could be done. The prince could not go and see his beloved, who was most miffed at being ignored, and no one could come and visit for the serpent prince guarded the roads and drove away all who traveled. No balls or feasts could be held, and the halls of the castle were shadowed and quiet.

Only the hissing of the serpent prince could be heard as he slipped and slithered through the empty streets.

Flora, the gardener's daughter, was very sorry to see her old friend so unhappy. He had always been such a merry boy, but now he moped about, miserable as the day was long. It pained her to see her old friend so unhappy. One day she went walking in the forest and came to a dark pool of water, shadowed by the gnarled branches of an ancient thorn tree. She sat beneath the tree, and a few tears slipped down her face and fell into the water, rippling the pool's still surface.

An old woman hobbled out of the tangled forest and asked her, "Why do you look so sad, pretty lass?"

The gardener's daughter said, "It's no use my telling you, for nobody in the world can help me."

"One never knows," said the old woman. "Tell me your trouble. Maybe I can help?"

Flora looked up in sudden hope. "I am just sorry for my old friend, the prince, who wishes to marry but cannot till his elder brother, the serpent prince, takes a bride for himself."

"You could marry the serpent yourself," the old woman said.

The girl started in horror. "But the beast would devour me!"

"Not if you do exactly what I say," the old woman said.

Flora stared at her, troubled. She did not want to marry the serpent prince, but she could think of no other way to help her friend. And her warm heart was touched by the plight of the poor creature, condemned to lurk in the shadows while his younger brother had everything a prince could wish for.

"What would I have to do?" she asked at last, falteringly.

"You must agree to marry the serpent prince of your own free will," the old woman said. "Then, once the wedding is over and it is time for you to retire, you must ask to be dressed in seven snow-white shifts. Then ask for a tub full of water boiled with ashes, and a tub full of fresh white milk, and as many whips as a boy can carry. Have all these things brought to your bedchamber."

"But … what use are such things?"

"Just listen. When the serpent tells you to shed a shift, you must bid him to slough a skin. Then, when he has shed all of his skins, you must dip the whips in the water boiled with ashes and whip him with all of your strength. Next, wash him in the fresh milk. Then, lastly, you must take him and hold him still in your arms as long as you can."

Flora shuddered at the thought of holding the serpent, green as poison, cold as the tomb.

"Trust me, my dear," the old woman said in a gentle voice. "I promise you that if you do just as I have said, all will go well."

So Flora set her jaw, and agreed.

The old woman smiled at her, patted her hand reassuringly, then hobbled away into the forest. Flora walked slowly home, thinking over the old woman's words. She found the prince sitting in the garden, his head bent into his hands.

"Don't be so sad!" she cried. "I intend to marry your brother."

The prince jumped up, his face lighting in sudden hope, then shook his head. "I cannot let you do such a thing."

"It is not for you to choose," Flora answered.

"But … why?" the prince cried. "Why would you sacrifice yourself for me?"

"We are friends," she answered. "Besides, he is the elder son. If I marry him, one day I will be queen."

The prince laughed. "And a very good queen you would be too!" Then his face sobered. "But … he will devour you in a single bite!"

"I shan't let him," she said.

He shook his head in admiration of her bravery.

When the wedding day arrived, Flora was fetched in the royal carriage with the six white horses, and taken to the castle to be decked as a bride. She asked for seven snow-white shifts, and a tub of water boiled with ashes, a tub of fresh milk, and as many whips as a boy could carry in his arms. The lords and ladies in the castle thought, of course, that this was merely some bit of peasant superstition, all rubbish and nonsense. But the king said, "Let her have whatever she asks for."

The bride-to-be was dressed in a beautiful green gown, the color of a forest in springtime, and her hair was unbraided and left loose down her back. She wore a crown of flowers gathered by her father, who stood with her, not knowing whether to be proud or afraid.

The great hall where the wedding ceremony was to take place was crowded with people, all agog with curiosity to see the girl brave enough to marry the serpent prince. And when the doors opened and the great snake slithered in, a moan and a mutter rose from a thousand throats. Only Flora did not groan or grimace. She stood steadfast, and fixed her eyes on the writhing form of her bridegroom. He glided to her side and coiled himself till he was tall and thick as a pillar, green as poison, cold as the tomb.

After the serpent prince and the gardener's daughter were married, a great wedding feast was held, a banquet fit for the son of a king. When the feast was over, the bridegroom and bride were taken to their apartment, accompanied by a great procession of flaming torches and musicians serenading them with trumpets and flutes.

As soon as the door was shut, the serpent loomed over the girl and said, "Fair maiden, shed a shift!"

"Prince Serpent, slough a skin!" Flora answered him at once. Her knees were shaking, but she refused to show her fear. All her trust was placed in the advice of the old woman from the forest.

"No one has ever dared tell me what to do before!" he said in astonishment.

"I command you to do it now!" said she.

He stared at her coldly, then began to wriggle and writhe. He squirmed out of a long green snakeskin, which lay limply on the floor. Flora drew off her first shift, and spread it on top of the skin.

Again, the serpent commanded, "Fair maiden, shed a shift."

"Prince Serpent, slough a skin," she answered.

44

"Again, you dare to command me?" the serpent cried, rearing high in anger.

"Yes, again I command you," said she.

He began to struggle and squirm, and finally cast off the second skin. She covered it with her second shift.

Then the serpent said for the third time, "Fair maiden, shed a shift."

She answered him again, "Prince Serpent, slough a skin."

He was angrier than ever. "How dare you command me! I shall swallow you whole!" he cried, his slitted eyes red as coals. But the girl was not afraid. Once more she commanded him to do as she bade.

Soon there were seven green serpent skins lying on the floor, each of them covered with a snow-white shift. And the serpent was now red as blood, hot as hellfire. The girl dipped a whip in the water boiled with ashes, and whipped the serpent with all of her strength. He twisted and turned, shrieked and shouted, but the girl kept on whipping till all the ashy water was gone. The serpent now lay meekly on the floor, and he was now not much taller than she.

Tenderly she washed him in the fresh white milk, till he was pink as the dawn, warm as life. Then she put her arms around him and held him fast. He struggled against her, but she closed her eyes and did not let go. For a while, she felt sure he must break free of her grasp, for he was so strong and supple. But at last he calmed and gentled.

Strong arms slid about her waist, and a warm mouth pressed to hers. She opened her eyes. Beside her lay the handsomest young prince that anyone could wish to see. She kissed him back joyously.

As the dawn chorus filled the air with song, the crown prince and his new bride went hand in hand and smiling to greet the royal court. The head gardener wept with joy to see his daughter safe, and the king and the queen laughed with joy to see their eldest son returned to his natural human form. The younger prince cheered, and called for the gilded coach drawn by six milk-white horses, so that he could call on the girl he wished to make his bride.

So, there was soon another wedding, and festivals and banquets and merrymakings for days and days and weeks and weeks. No bride was ever so beloved by a king and queen as the girl from the gardener's cottage, for with her good sense and her courage, she had saved their son, Prince Serpent.

Kate says:

I had never read "A Bride For Me Before a Bride for You" before Lorena shared it with me, but it is now a favorite of mine. I love the way the girl stands up to the serpent and commands him to slough his skin!

Chosen by Lorena, who says:

"A Bride for Me Before a Bride for You" originated from a tale about the lindworm, a creature popular in Scandinavian mythology, which I adore for its darkness and unusual denouement. The tale is rich with archetypes and buried meanings: fertility symbols; our own duality; the shedding of skin. What stuck most in my mind was the singular bravery of the gardener's daughter, trudging up to the bridal chamber with buckets and whips in hand. I even have a soft spot for the terrifying serpent who, under all those scales and skins, is tender and helpless as a baby.

I love how Kate has given the gardener's daughter more autonomy in her retelling of the tale. In traditional versions, the girl is forced into a deadly marriage, and into fighting for her life, but here Kate has given her a bravery and intent that brings even more strength to an incredible fairy tale.

"The Rainbow Prince" tells the story of the adventures of a princess kidnapped by a wicked old fairy. The princess manages to save herself and a captive prince with the help of her little dog and cat. It was first published anonymously as "Le Prince Arc-en-ciel" in the French fairy tale collection *Nouveaux contes de fees* in 1718, and has been attributed to the Chevalier de Mailly, thought to have died in 1724. It was included, under the title "Fairer-than-a-Fairy," by Andrew Lang in *The Yellow Fairy Book* in 1894.

The Rainbow Prince

Once, in a kingdom far, far away, there lived a king and queen who had no children for many years. At last a baby girl was born to them, and she was so remarkably beautiful that the royal couple named her "Fairer-than-a-Fairy."

It didn't occur to the king and queen that such a name might make the fairies jealous. But, unfortunately, as soon as the fairies heard of the princess's presumptuous name, they resolved to punish her parents.

The eldest of the fairies was entrusted to carry out their revenge. Her name was Lagree, and she was so old that she only had one eye and one tooth left. She was also so spiteful that she gladly devoted all her time to carrying out all the ill-natured tricks of the whole kingdom of fairies.

One day, when Fairer-than-a-Fairy was playing with her dog and her cat in the castle garden, Lagree swooped down in a whirl of black smoke and spitting cinders. The little princess was then only seven years old, and she screamed at the sight of the hideous old creature. Lagree put her bony hand over the princess's mouth and together they spun away into the sky. Fairer-than-a-Fairy struggled desperately to be free. She looked down at the castle, and saw – to her great relief – that her dog and her cat were racing behind, their eyes fixed upon her.

Knowing that her pets were following was a comfort to the poor little princess. When the old fairy landed in the courtyard of a tall tower with high walls and iron gates, Fairer-than-a-Fairy kept her head high. "You must take me home," she said. "My parents will be so worried."

"Never!" the old fairy cackled. "You are mine now, and must do as I say."

She led Fairer-than-a-Fairy inside the shadowed hall of the tower. A fire blazed on the hearth, and there was one huge bed so high it needed steps to climb into it. Two crystal bottles stood on a chest next to it, both filled with liquid with a strange shifting gleam.

"Watch this fire!" Lagree ordered. "If it ever goes out, it shall be the worse for you!"

Fairer-than-a-Fairy had never tended a fire before, but gamely she bent to poke the fire and add some more kindling. The old fairy ordered her to cook dinner, and clean up afterwards. The princess did as she was told, as well as she could.

Then the wicked old fairy climbed up into the bed.

"Pass me one of those bottles," she ordered. Fairer-than-a-Fairy obeyed, and the old witch yanked at her single tooth till it came free of her gum. She dropped it into the bottle, and shut it with a glass stopper. Her tooth bobbed up and down inside the bottle, curved and yellow and cruel.

"Pass me the other bottle," Lagree ordered. The princess did as she was told, and the old fairy plucked her single eye from its socket. Groping blindly, she dropped it into the bottle and stoppered it firmly. Her eye bounced up and down inside the bottle, round and staring and rude.

"Take care of these bottles!" Lagree ordered. "They contain a special magical liquid to make my eye and my tooth sharp and strong. If the bottles should ever break and the liquid spill, it shall be the worse for you!"

Fairer-than-a-Fairy put the bottles back on the chest, trying not to look at what was inside. There was nowhere for her to lie down except on a tattered old rug by the fire, and so she curled up there and wept herself to sleep.

In the morning, the wicked fairy demanded the bottles be brought to her, and she put her eye back in its socket and her tooth back in her mouth. "Watch the fire! Guard the bottles!

Else it'll be the worse for you," she shouted, then disappeared in a swirl of smoke and cinders.

The little princess was left alone. With her heart beating uncomfortably fast, she crept out and explored the tower. Everything was vast and empty and echoing. Fairer-than-a-Fairy felt more alone and afraid than she ever had before. She went outside and found a small overgrown garden. A fountain stood in the middle of the garden, its waters muddy and dark. Its spout was clogged with slime, and the princess cleaned it out so the water could run freely. It made her happy to see the sparkling water begin to play, and she cleared dead leaves from the bowl so it had somewhere to flow.

Just then, the princess heard a mewling and a meowing above her head. She looked up, and saw her slim black cat slinking along the outer wall. Crying out in delight, she held out her arms. Her cat leapt down, and Fairer-than-a-Fairy held her close, rubbing her cheek on the cat's soft fur.

Then the princess heard a scrape and a scrabble at the gateway. She bent down, and saw her dog's black nose snuffling under the gate. He dug furiously. Soon he had tunneled under the gate and was prancing happily at the princess's heels. Fairer-than-a-Fairy played with her pets all afternoon, and then – when Lagree returned – they warned her by running to hide in the shadows. With only one eye, the fairy did not see them and the animals were careful to keep hidden.

If it had not been for her pets, Fairer-than-a-Fairy would have been lonely and unhappy. No one came to the fortress except the wicked old fairy, and the princess had to do all the cleaning and cooking by herself, as well as cut wood for the fire, and make sure the crystal bottles were always safe. But Lagree was rarely there during the day, so Fairer-than-a-Fairy could dig weeds from the garden, play with her pets, and read her way through the books on the shelves.

The days passed, and then the months, and then the years. Fairer-than-a-Fairy grew into a beautiful young woman, and over time forgot all about the court of the king, her father.

In the little walled garden, the fountain flung up handfuls of shining water all day long, and bees hummed in the flowers. Fairer-than-a-Fairy loved to sit beside the fountain, paddling her bare feet in the cool water and listening to the tinkle of the falling droplets. Her dog would swim in the bowl, then shake his wet fur and shower her, while the little cat liked to pat the glittering surface of the water and dream about catching the fish that lurked beneath the water lilies.

One day Fairer-than-a-Fairy sat dabbling her fingers in the water. The sun struck through the falling veil of water and created a brilliant rainbow. Fairer-than-a-Fairy leaned forward in delight. Suddenly a young man's voice sounded in her head. "Oh, if only she knew how much joy she brings me! A dozen years I've been trapped in this rainbow, with no one to speak to and no one to care. If only she could hear me."

"Who is it that speaks?" Fairer-than-a-Fairy cried.

The rainbow replied in a tone of surprise and wonderment. "I have been so long a prisoner that I can scarcely remember my name. All I know is that I am a prince, and the oldest and wickedest of the fairies stole me from my family in revenge for some imagined wrongdoing."

"I also!" Fairer-than-a-Fairy exclaimed. "We are prisoners together."

She nicknamed him Prince Rainbow. From that moment onwards, the two captives met every day to talk, and share memories, and wonder about the future. The prince only appeared when the sun struck through the falling water at the perfect angle to make a rainbow, and so Fairer-than-a-Fairy was sad when the sky was cloudy or when dusk fell.

Soon she thought about the imprisoned prince all the time, and she began to daydream and take less care in her daily chores. One evening, flushed and happy from the garden and a long talk with Prince Rainbow, Fairer-than-a-Fairy realized she had forgotten to tend the fire. She stared at the pile of cold gray ashes in the hearth in dismay. Her dog sat beside her, his ears sunk low and his tail tucked between his legs, while the little cat mewled in distress.

The ashes began to stir and spin. The animals fled, whimpering, into the shadows. The old fairy Lagree rose up out of the dead fire, smoke and sparks whirling from her black skirts. "You have failed!" she shrieked, pointing her bony finger at the cowering princess. "A small task I left you. An easy task! But no. Too hard a chore for such a stupid princess as you."

Fairer-than-a-Fairy stammered an apology, but Lagree did not listen. "At dawn, you must head west into the forest and find the castle of the ogre. You must beg from him a live coal to relight this fire."

"An … an ogre?" Fairer-than-a-Fairy faltered. "But … will he not wish to eat me?"

"I daresay he will," Lagree answered with a cruel smile. "It is nothing more than you deserve."

The next morning, Fairer-than-a-Fairy rose at dawn. The sun was only just peeking above the horizon, and so the fountain did not shine with rainbows. She lingered there for a moment, wishing that she could say farewell to the prince and afraid she would never see him again.

The gate stood ajar for the first time in ten years, and Fairer-than-a-Fairy slipped into the forest, her legs trembling with trepidation. The forest was calm, however, and a bird sang sweetly. With her warm cat purring in her arms, and her little dog gamboling at her heels, the princess headed west, taking courage in the beauty of the day.

As she crossed over a rushing brook, the bird in the trees sang to her:

"Shine bright, full of light, shine clear, no need to fear."

A spark of light caught her eye. Fairer-than-a-Fairy bent and picked up a shining pebble out of the water. It was like a tiny rainbow in her hand, and she carried it eagerly, thinking of the prince in the fountain and wondering if he would miss her when she did not come that day.

By sunset, she had come to the ogre's castle, a dark and dreadful place. Gnawed bones lay scattered on either side of the road and the bridge was made of skulls. The moat was slimy and stinking. Sunlight would never spark a rainbow there.

Fairer-than-a-Fairy was gathering together her courage to cross the bridge of skulls, when her cat jumped up onto her shoulder, black fur all on end, hissing and spitting. Her little dog seized the hem of her dress and dragged her back from the road. Fairer-than-a-Fairy hid in the shadows of the forest, just as a huge ogre with gnashing teeth like rusty saws stomped over the bridge.

"Hie-hoh, hie-hoh, it's a-hunting I go! Crack her bones, hear her groan, eat her flesh, sweet and fresh. Hie-hoh, hie-hoh, it's a-killing I go!"

The ground shuddered under his enormous feet, and the trees swished and swayed. Fairer-than-a-Fairy waited till the ogre was out of sight, then tiptoed across the bridge of skulls and into the ogre's castle.

Her skin rose in goose bumps as she walked into the cold darkness. With her cat and her dog at her heels, Fairer-than-a-Fairy crept across the floor, not knowing where to go. Then the pebble in her hand caught a spark of golden light. The princess looked ahead, and saw a dim line of red under a wooden door as tall as a cliff. She tiptoed forward and eased through the crack, finding herself in a dark, cavernous kitchen. A giant ogress sat in a rocking chair by the fire, weeping. A waterfall of tears rolled down her face, and splashed onto the flagstones below.

The princess stood on tiptoe, and shouted up at the ogress, "Whatever is the matter?"

The ogress looked around in surprise. Fairer-than-a-Fairy waved her handkerchief, and eventually the ogress looked down and saw her. She jumped up onto her chair and shrieked.

"Please don't be afraid, I mean you no harm," Fairer-than-a-Fairy said. "Why are you crying?"

"My husband goes off every night a-hunting and a-killing, instead of staying home to keep me company," the ogress said, with a sigh so gusty it blew all the princess's skirts up.

"I know what it's like to be lonely," Fairer-than-a-Fairy said, offering the ogress her handkerchief. "I'll keep you company."

The ogress took the handkerchief between the tips of two fingers and dabbed it to her eyes. Then she lifted the princess up onto the table so they could play a round of backgammon together, though Fairer-than-a-Fairy needed to exert all her strength to roll the pieces about on the board. They ate a fine supper, and told each other stories till it was midnight.

"You had best go now," the ogress said sadly, as the giant clock on the mantelpiece clanged loudly. "My husband will be home soon."

"May I have a coal from your fire?" Fairer-than-a-Fairy asked, holding up the tin bucket she had brought. "I have little to give you in return. Only this pretty pebble." She showed the shining stone to the ogress.

"Bless your sweet heart, you keep the pebble. It'll come in useful, I am sure. Here's a coal for you, in thanks for keeping me company tonight."

The ogress took up a giant pair of tongs, removed a flaming coal from the fire and dropped it in the princess's bucket. It was so huge and hot and heavy, Fairer-than-a-Fairy was afraid she could not lift up the bucket.

"Hie-hoh, hie-hoh," the ogre sang as he stamped home through the night.

Fairer-than-a-Fairy heaved up the bucket with all her strength and carried it out into the forest as fast as she could, her pets running beside her. She hurried through the dark forest, the shining pebble lighting her way, and was back at the fairy's tower by sunrise.

Lagree was most dumbfounded to see her, and disgruntled too. But Fairer-than-a-Fairy simply carried the great glowing coal to the fire, heaved it onto the cold ashes, and quickly built

up the fire again. The old fairy showed her displeasure by making the princess scrub the tower from cellar to attic, and wash every sheet, pillowcase and handkerchief in the place. Although, Fairer-than-a-Fairy was so tired she could scarcely keep her eyes open, she sang as she worked for she was alive when she had feared she must die.

The next day, when the sun struck the wall at the perfect angle, she ran to tell Prince Rainbow all that had befallen. Her step was light and dancing, her eyes bright with joy, and she held out her hands to the rainbow, wishing she could touch his fingers with hers.

Unbeknown to her, Lagree had hidden herself behind the wall. The old fairy heard and saw all that went on between the princess and prince. In a great rage, she jumped out and conjured up a black spinning funnel of smoke and lightning which smote the fountain and cracked it in two. The water spilt and drained away. The rainbow faded. The last words the princess heard were, "Fairer-than-a-Fairy, I love you!" Then the prince's voice faded away too. Fairer-than-a-Fairy sobbed and hid her face in her hands, as Lagree cackled in malicious glee.

When the old fairy had whirled herself away, the princess went slowly inside. Each step was heavy, and her heart ached. She sat in the window seat and wept. Her little black dog came and sat by her feet and her little black cat crept into her lap, both doing their best to comfort her.

Then Fairer-than-a-Fairy heard her name being whispered. She looked up, and saw the two crystal bottles on the chest. A long finger of sunlight touched the edge of one of the bottles. The faintest of rainbows hung in the air beyond.

"Prince Rainbow?"

"I'm here."

She grabbed both bottles in her hands, setting them in the window. The light slanted through the magical gleaming liquid within, and refracted into a glimmering double rainbow of many colors. In the space between, she saw a young man smiling at her. His hair was the color of sunlight, his eyes the color of water.

"My darling Fairer-than-a-Fairy," he whispered. "Lagree does not realize it, but when she broke the fountain she broke the spell. I am trapped in the rainbow no longer. However, I am sick and hurt. You must come to me and bring me the bottles of enchanted water, so that I may heal and grow strong."

"How am I to find you?" Fairer-than-a-Fairy cried.

"Follow the light of the rainbow stone," he whispered.

The princess did not hesitate. Carefully, she wrapped the two bottles in her shawl and put them in a basket, then, with her pets at her heels and the rainbow stone showing her the way, set out into the forest to save her dearest prince.

When the old fairy Lagree became aware of her prisoner's flight she was furious, and set off in pursuit as fast as she could. She moved so fast a whirlwind sprang up at her heels, a vortex of spinning dirt and leaves and twigs. Fairer-than-a-Fairy sprang behind a tree. Her little dog rushed out and barked furiously at the old fairy. Lagree got such a fright she tripped over, and broke her only tooth against a stone.

Fairer-than-a-Fairy ran on at full speed. But Lagree did not give up. She caught up with the exhausted princess just as the sun was going down.

"I've got you now!" she cackled, seizing Fairer-than-a-Fairy's arm with both of her long-taloned hands. But the little cat sprang down onto Lagree's head from a branch. The old fairy got such a fright she leapt back, and pierced her only eye with a thorn. Blind and bleeding, Lagree could not go on.

Fairer-than-a-Fairy limped onwards, following the rainbow stone's path. At last she came upon a wonderful silver castle suspended by strong silver chains from the branches of four immense and ancient oak trees. It rocked slightly in the breeze. A long ladder made of silver rope dangled down to the ground, swaying from side to side.

Fairer-than-a-Fairy climbed up the ladder into the castle. Inside, a vast hall was lit by glittering stars in the ceiling. Prince Rainbow lay on a couch in the middle of the room, looking pale and thin and weak. Fairer-than-a-Fairy knelt beside him, and unstoppered one of the little crystal bottles. She held it to his lips, and tipped in some of the magical strengthening liquid. His lips moved, and he swallowed. Color rose to his cheeks. The princess supported him, as he drank the rest of the liquid, and then she unstoppered the second bottle. Prince Rainbow sat up, and drank the second bottle all on his own. Then he smiled at Fairer-than-a-Fairy, and kissed her tenderly.

"You've saved me!" he cried. "Will you marry me?"

"Of course," Fairer-than-a-Fairy replied.

So, they were married at the castle of Fairer-than-a-Fairy's parents. Her little black dog and her little black cat walked before her, each with a golden ring tied about their necks with a golden ribbon. No one could have loved each other more than Fairer-than-a-Fairy and her Prince Rainbow.

And old, eyeless, toothless Lagree was never heard from again.

Chosen by Kate, who says:

I remember reading this tale – then titled "Fairer-than-a-Fairy" – in Andrew Lang's *The Yellow Fairy Book* when I was a little girl, and loved the fact that her dog and her cat helped her triumph. The original story was rather long, so I cut it back to its essentials while bringing Fairer-than-a-Fairy's courage and cleverness to the fore.

In other tales in this book, we have chosen to use the spelling "faery" as it seemed to conjure the tall, dangerous, otherworldly creatures of the Fae better than "fairy," which seems to connote beings that are both tiny and benign. However, in this story we have kept the more usual spelling to maintain the linkage between "fairer" and "fairy" in the heroine's name.

Lorena says:

I adore Kate's version of "Fairer-than-a-Fairy," and the wonderful images her writing conjured up in my mind: the Prince, hidden in the fountain, yet just visible in the rainbow; the wonderful bridge of skulls; the witch's eye and tooth, kept safe in their bottles; the castle, hanging high in the green forest.

When I was first working on the illustrations, we had some visiting friends return from a walk with a silk scarf wrapped in a bundle. They announced, "We brought you a present!" and unveiled a pile of dried bones. A whole fox skeleton! You may think it an odd present, but it shows that they know me all too well. I was thrilled, and knew immediately that it would form the bridge of skulls.

"The Singing, Springing Lark" is a beautiful variant of the well-known "Beauty and the Beast" tale in which the heroine must follow a trail of blood and white feathers left by her beast-husband for seven years, before outwitting the enchantress who had cursed him. It is an oral tale told to Wilhelm Grimm by his future wife, Dortchen Wild, in 1814 and was included in the Grimm brothers' 2nd edition of tales in 1815.

The Singing, Springing Lark

Once upon a time there was a man who was about to set forth on a long journey. He asked his three daughters what gifts he could bring for them on his return. The oldest daughter wanted diamonds, the second daughter wanted rubies, but the third one said, "Father dear, I would like a singing, springing lark." .

"If I can find one, I shall bring it home for you," he promised. He kissed his three daughters farewell and went on his way.

At last, after many adventures, the father began his journey home. He had bought diamonds and rubies for his two oldest daughters, but he had searched everywhere in vain for a singing, springing lark. This made him very sad, for his youngest daughter was his favorite child.

His path home led him through a dark and tangled forest. Through the brambles and briars, he saw the shape of a great stone castle, all hung with ivy and cobwebs.

His horse began to snort and fret. Then it reared, throwing the man to the ground. It galloped off into the gloom, leaving him lying alone on the ground, his breath knocked out of him.

The air was filled with the sweetest singing he had ever heard. He looked up. Flying high in the sky above him was a lark. The little bird dipped down and perched in a branch right above his head.

"Aha! A singing, springing lark! You are just what I have been looking for," the man said.

The man got up and began to climb the tree to try and catch the bird. But then a great lion leapt out of the shadows and roared till the leaves on the trees trembled. "I will devour anyone who tries to steal my singing, springing lark!"

The man was so startled that he fell out of the tree, and lay on the ground, right under the lion's roaring jaws.

"I did not know the lark belonged to you," the man cried. "Please spare me!"

The lion growled menacingly and said,

"Nothing can save you unless you promise to give
me the first living creature that greets you
when you arrive home."

The man hesitated. "That could be my youngest daughter. She loves me the most, and always runs to meet me when I return home." But then he looked at the great and terrible lion standing over him, and thought to himself, *Perhaps it shall be the cat who greets me.*

And so he agreed, and the lion allowed him to leave the forest, with the singing, springing lark imprisoned in a cage.

The man hoped with all his heart that it would be the cat who ran to greet him when he arrived home. But it was his beloved youngest daughter, Lullala. She threw her arms around him and kissed him, exclaiming with joy at the sight of the little bird.

The man was racked with horror and guilt. He fell to his knees and put his arms about her waist. "Alas, Lullala, my dearest child, I've had to pay a high price for this bird. I had to promise you to a wild lion and when he gets you, he'll tear you to pieces and eat you up."

When she heard the story, however, Lullala said, "Dearest father, your promise must be kept. I will go to the lion. If he can talk, perhaps he is not such a wild and savage beast. Perhaps I can persuade him not to tear me to pieces."

So, summoning up all her courage, the girl went into the dark and tangled forest, to the castle all hung with ivy and cobwebs, carrying the cage with the singing, springing lark. It took

her a long time to walk there, and the sun was setting behind the castle towers. Her stomach was knotted with fear, and her hands shook. No lion leapt out of the shadows to devour her, however. All was still and quiet.

Lullala tiptoed into the castle. In the dimming twilight, she found a great hall set with golden plates and goblets, brimming over with food and wine. But there was no fire lit on the hearth, and no candles in the candelabra. Greatly wondering, the girl ate and drank, and by the time she had finished, the room was so dark she could not see her hands before her face.

Then the deep voice of a young man spoke out of the shadows.

"Thank you for coming. Do not be afraid. I mean you no harm."

"Who are you?" the girl said in a voice that quavered.

"I am the prince of this castle. Once it was a merry place, filled with laughter and music. But then I was cursed by an evil enchantress, after I refused to marry her. By day, I am transformed into a wild lion. I am only returned to my natural shape at night, and I must take care that no light of any kind falls upon me, for then I shall be turned into a dove and forced to fly about the world for seven years."

The girl was filled with pity at this story. "We must make sure that no light falls upon you then," she said.

The prince said incredulously, "Then you will stay?"

"Yes," she answered, and put out her hand to find him in the darkness.

So, the girl married the enchanted prince and stayed with him in the castle. By day, she combed the lion's golden mane, listening to the sweet song of the singing, springing lark. By night, she lay in her prince's arms, discovering love.

One day word came to her that her eldest sister was to be married. The girl greatly wished to see her family again, and so the lion escorted her to the edge of the forest and she ran all the way home. Her father and sisters were overjoyed to see her again, and were full of questions about the lion.

"Is he not cruel and fearsome?" the eldest sister asked.

"Is he not terrible and fierce?" the second sister said.

"Do you not wish to come home?" her father said.

"My husband is good and kind," Lullala said. "And I am happy and well. I do not want any other life."

But in her secret heart she wished that she knew how to break the enchantment.

After the wedding Lullala returned home, and her life at the old castle resumed. But she missed her family, and wished that she could introduce her husband to them. When news came, some time later, that her second eldest sister was to be married too, Lullala begged the lion prince to go with her and meet her family.

"It is too dangerous," he told her. "Remember, if even the faintest thread of light was to touch me when I am in my human form, I shall be transformed into a dove, and must fly about the world for seven years."

But the girl promised to keep him safe from any light, and so the lion consented to go. In the dead of night, they traveled through the forest, in a carriage without any lamps or linkmen, its windows blacked out with thick cloth. When they arrived, the prince was muffled in a great cloak and hurried down to a room prepared for them in the deepest, darkest cellar of the house.

There, in pitch blackness, he met his father-in-law and shook his hand and congratulated the two elder sisters on their marriage. The girl's family were filled with wonder and worry in equal parts, at this man who must live always in shadows.

Then the girl kissed her husband goodbye, and went with her family to the wedding feast. There was much merriment and dancing, and the girl wished with all her heart that her husband could celebrate with her. Afterwards, the wedding party walked back to the merchant's house in a long procession lit by flaming torches. After bidding all good night, Lullala felt her way down to the cellar, stumbling through the darkness as if she was blind.

But as she opened the door, she heard the frantic beating of wings and felt wind blowing about her face. She cried out in alarm.

"Light found its way to me," her husband cried, in the high, thin voice of a bird. "For seven years I must fly about the world. Every seven steps I shall let fall a drop of red blood and one white feather. Follow me! Try to save me."

Without another word the dove flew out the door, and she ran after him. Every seven steps, a single drop of red glistening blood and a single white feather fell, showing her the way.

She followed till her dress hung in rags about her.

She followed till her shoes were worn through, and her feet were torn and bruised.

She followed until nothing was left of her but shadows and bone.

For seven years she followed her beloved, till one day no little feather and no drop of red blood fell. When she raised her eyes, the dove had disappeared.

The girl fell to her knees in despair, thinking she had lost the trail of her beloved. But Lullala took courage and said, "I will continue on as far as the wind blows and as long as the cock crows, until I find him."

She raised her eyes to the skies, and saw there the great burning disc of the sun.

Lullala cried:

"Sun, you shine into every crack and over every peak. Have you seen a white dove flying?"

"No," said the sun, "I have not seen the white dove, but I will give you this little chest. Open it when you are in great need."

She thanked the sun and went on until evening came and the moon was shining. She asked the moon, "Moon, you shine all night, across the fields and the seas. Have you seen a white dove flying?"

"No," said the moon, "I have not seen the white dove, but I will give you this magical egg. Break it open when you are in great need."

Lullala thanked the moon and went on until the wind blew against her. She said to it, "Wind, you blow over every tree and under every leaf. Have you seen a white dove flying?"

"Yes," said the wind, "I have seen your white dove. He is now a man again, for the seven years are over. He is under a spell cast by the wicked enchantress who first cursed him. They are to marry three days hence."

The poor girl wept. She had followed her beloved so far and for so long, and it hurt her cruelly to know that he was to marry another. But she dashed away her tears and took a deep breath, determined to do her best to save her beloved.

Then the wind said to her, "Do not despair. You have the gifts of the sun and the moon, and now I shall give you another. Here is a little wooden flute. Blow on it when you are in great need, and I will send help."

So, Lullala limped on and on in her ragged dress until she came to a great castle. Crowds of people dressed in all their finery were preparing for a great feast to begin the wedding festivities.

The girl opened the little chest that the sun had given her. Inside, a golden dress glowed like the sun itself. She dressed herself in it, then went up into the castle. The prince did not see her. He stared blank faced at nothing. But everyone else, even the bride herself, gazed at her in astonishment.

"I want that dress!" the enchantress cried. "I must have it. Give it to me."

"Not for coins or jewels," answered the girl, "but for flesh and blood."

"What do you mean?" the enchantress demanded.

The girl answered, "Let me sleep one night in the room where the bridegroom sleeps."

The bride did not want to allow this, but she wanted the golden dress very much. So, she agreed, but then secretly she twisted the glowing ring upon her finger and tipped some white powder into the prince's wine cup.

That night the girl was led into the room where the prince slept. She sat down on the bed and said, "I followed you for seven years. I begged news of you from the sun and the moon and the wind. Have you forgotten me?"

But the prince did not wake. He did not hear her.

The next morning, the girl gave the golden dress to the enchantress. The prince did not notice. He stared blank faced at nothing.

Dressed again in her rags, the girl sat and wept. At last, though, she gathered up her courage again and broke open the egg. Inside were ropes of pearls, each gleaming like tiny moons.

The girl hung the pearls about her throat and went back to the palace.

"I want those pearls!" the enchantress cried. "I must have them. Give them to me."

"Not for coins or jewels, but for flesh and blood," the girl answered. "Let me sleep one night in the room where the bridegroom sleeps."

The bride agreed, intending to give him another sleeping potion. But this time, the girl watched carefully. She took the goblet of wine the enchantress gave to the prince, and swapped it with the enchantress's goblet.

That night, the girl sat on the prince's bed and said, "I followed you for seven years. I begged news of you from the sun and the moon and the wind. Have you forgotten me?"

The prince opened his eyes, and gazed at her joyously. "My dearest," he cried, embracing her. "You have saved me! Now the curse will be broken and I will be beast no longer."

They leapt up, ready to flee the castle, but the enchantress burst in, eyes flaming with anger. She raised her wand to strike them down, but the girl quickly lifted the wooden flute to her mouth and blew. As the sweet notes rang out, the wind sprung up and knocked the enchantress, heels over head, head over heels, all the way down the stairs.

Then the wind transformed himself into the shape of a rainbow-winged griffin. The girl and her beloved leapt onto his back, and together they soared away into the rose-blushed morning sky and flew all the way home to their castle in the woods.

From that time on, they lived happily until they died, listening together to the sweet music of the singing, springing lark.

Chosen by Kate, who says:

I first read "The Singing, Springing Lark" while I was writing my novel *The Wild Girl,* inspired by the true story of the forbidden romance between Wilhelm Grimm and Dortchen Wild. I loved it at once and knew that I wanted to retell it in some way. I have now done so twice.

The first retelling occurred as I prepared the tale for an oral storytelling performance (I tell stories as well as write them). I simplified the pattern of action and added detail and dialogue. It is this version of the story that you have just read. I also made a few changes to the story for dramatic effect, such as adding in the enchantress's poison ring and making the gift from the moon being strings of pearls instead of a gold mechanical hen with twelve chicks.

The second time I drew upon "The Singing, Springing Lark" was in my historical novel *The Beast's Garden*, which retells the tale set in the underground resistance to Hitler in Nazi Germany.

Lorena says:

While creating the illustrations for this book, I decided early on that the humans would be solid figures, made of *themselves,* while the creatures, born of imagination, are formed from the scraps of the places they inhabit. The lion in this story, like several other creatures in these pages, was created with sticks, leaves, bones … detritus from the forest floor.

Most of the girls and women represented in these pages are my daughters Mari and Rosa, but in "The Singing, Springing Lark," it is Kate's daughter Ella who has the starring role. Kate and I communicated by email for a couple of years before she flew down to visit with Ella, so I could photograph her for the illustrations. How wonderful it is for us both to have our daughters in this book. It makes it a very special project for both of us.

"The Stolen Child" is the story of a young woman who braves the wicked faery folk of the Sidhe to win back her stolen baby. It is a Scottish oral folktale originally collected and retold by Sorche Nic Leodhas in her Newbery Honor-winning book *Thistle and Thyme: Tales & Legends from Scotland*, 1962.

The Stolen Child

One wild stormy evening in the Scottish Highlands, two fishermen saw the crumpled figure of a fallen woman on the shore, lashed by rain and the spray of the wild sea.

"'Tis a lass!" said the younger of the two.

"Don't even think of stopping for the girl," said the other, looking in fear at the sea crashing all about them. "Our boat will break to pieces!"

"But look – she's like a fallen angel," said the first. "We cannot go home and have our dinner knowing we left her behind!"

So, the two fishermen carefully brought their boat in to the cliffs and the younger one climbed up the wet slippery rocks to the lass. He lifted her over his shoulder and, with great difficulty, brought her down to the boat.

"Is she still with us?" he asked anxiously, bending over her.

"Aye," said the other, "but we'd best get her back to the village right quick."

They rowed home and carried her ashore, her wet hair hanging down like golden seaweed. The women of the village wrapped her in warm blankets, and rubbed her cold limbs with linen towels. They lifted a cup of hot tea made from fern roots and honey to her white lips. The lass drank a little, and coughed and, at last, opened her eyes.

"My bairn," she murmured. "Where's my bairn?"

"My dear," said one old woman, glancing worriedly at the other womenfolk. "You were found quite alone."

The lass sat up straight, surprising them all. "Nay! I bundled my bairn good and safe by the path while I went to fetch him water. I must have tripped and fallen down the cliff! My bairn must still be there!"

With haste, the villagers formed a search team and returned to the cliffs. They searched all night and all day, looking behind every rock and bush, and climbing up and down the cliffs. But there was no sign of a lost baby.

Nothing could comfort the poor young mother. She started up from her sickbed, a sob in her throat, and tried to dash out into the rain. The young fisherman who had carried her down the cliffs caught her hand. "Please don't go! It's not safe. Stay here with us."

The old woman looked at him shrewdly before adding, "This can be your home now. We have many a fine lad for you to marry. You'll have another bairn before long, no doubt."

The lass – whose name was Rosemary - drew in her breath.

"Thank you just the same, I know you mean well.
But now I am going to go and find my bairn."

Rosemary traveled from croft to croft, from village to village, searching and asking everyone she met about her lost baby. With her hair blown about and a wild expression in her eyes, many thought her crazed. Perhaps she was, a little.

One day the forlorn lass wandered into a camp of Gypsies. A brightly colored caravan was pulled close to a small fire, where a woman in a long, ragged skirt stood stirring an iron pot. Children sat whittling toys and tools out of wood, while a long-haired man sat fixing a pile of pots and pans.

"Where is my bairn? I've lost my little boy. Can anyone help me?" Rosemary begged, thin hands stretched out imploringly. "Have you seen my boy?"

The woman laid down her long wooden spoon.

"Alas, I have not," said the Gypsy. "But my grandmother is the wisest woman I know. If anyone can help you find your little one, it is she."

She led the lass towards the fire, where an old woman sat hunched upon a fallen log, her eyes misted over with blindness. She was dressed in layers of bright patched skirts, with tarnished coins hanging about her neck and sewn within the knots of her hair. Saying nothing, the grandmother clasped her hands upon the hands of the lass and there they sat, hour after hour, hand in hand, till darkness fell.

At midnight, the grandmother scattered a handful of herbs over the fire. The fire leapt up. Smoke swirled round the old Gypsy's head. She closed her eyes and listened. When the fire died down, she took the lass's hand again.

"Give up your search, poor lass," she said sorrowfully, "for your baby has been stolen away by the Sìdh. Taken to live with the faeries, he was. It's best that you accept it. The Sìdh are far more powerful than we mortals."

Rosemary was silent. Then she said darkly, "If I cannot get back my bairn, I might as well lay down and die."

"No, child!" urged the old Gypsy. "Perhaps there is a way …"

"What?" whispered the lass. "A spell?"

"Ah, if only it were that easy!" said the Gypsy. "The Sìdh love all things of beauty. If you take them a gift of rare and extraordinary loveliness, they will want it. Perhaps then you could bargain with them. But it would have to be something without equal anywhere in the world. And I'm afraid you would need two such treasures – one to gain entrance to the hollow hills where the Sìdh live, and another to bargain for your babe."

Tears filled the young mother's eyes. She had nothing – not even shoes to protect her feet or a shawl to keep out the cold. How could she bargain for her baby's life with nothing?

The old woman sighed. "What's more, the time for you to obtain two such treasures is short. If only you had ten years! But in ten days the people of the Sìdh gather together in their underground palace to choose a new ruler for the next hundred years. Your baby is sure to be among those that gather. After that, who knows where your babe might be?"

Rosemary looked down at her white-clasped hands. Tears ran unchecked down her thin face.

"There is one thing I can do for you," the Gypsy said. The old woman laid one gnarled hand upon her head and cast a spell to protect her from fire and earth, wind and water. "Now rest here with me," she said.

The lass shook her head.

"I will not rest till I have found my bairn."

"Then know this," the old Gypsy said. "It is not easy to find a gateway into the Otherworld. You must look for a thorn tree by a narrow cave in a hill of perfect symmetry, or a tree with a doorway in its hollowed-out trunk, no matter how small. Look for a crossroad that leads into water, or a circle of old stones that faces the sun, or a fairy ring of toadstools, or a grove of seven trees entwined."

Rosemary nodded, though her heart beast faster in fear.

"And remember," the old woman said, "the gateways of the Sìdh are always set at the thresholds of worlds, and can only be crossed at the times between times. At dawn or dusk, midnight or noon, moonrise or moonset, and the time between winter and summer."

The lass thanked the old Gypsy, and went on through the woods, her head whirling. She had nothing but her own bare hands and feet, her own eyes and mouth, her own golden hair. How could she, penniless as a beggar, obtain a rare and wondrous treasure? How could she obtain two?

Rosemary remembered the old stories her grandmother used to tell her, of the legendary wonders of the kings of yesteryear. Stories of the famous white cloak of King Nechtan, and the golden stringed harp of King Wrad. Suddenly the lass knew what she must do.

She headed straight to the sea, to the shore where the eider ducks nested and left behind the soft down of their breasts. She clambered up and down the rocks, gathering the delicate white feathers. The rocks did not cut her. The sun did not burn her. The bushes did not scratch her. She was under the old Gypsy's spell of protection, and she was filled with gratitude.

When Rosemary had gathered all the eiderdown she could find, she wove a cloak so soft and thick it looked as if a cloud had been plucked from the sky. Then she wound her long golden hair about one hand. With her little knife, she chopped it all off. Setting aside one thick curling lock, she used the rest of her hair to embroider golden flowers and leaves all over the cloak. Day and night she worked, for there was not a moment to lose.

After Rosemary had laid the final stitch, she carefully folded the soft white cloak, hid it under a shrub of gorse and returned to the seashore. Searching the beach, she looked for the right shape of bones to make a frame for a harp. The pebbles did not bruise her. The wind did not chill her. The waves did not sweep her away. Once again, the lass was grateful to the Gypsy's spell which kept her safe from harm.

Then she found an arch of bone that had been washed by the waves to such a smooth perfection that it resembled ivory. Taking the bone back to the shrub of gorse, she tied it together to make a frame for a harp. From the lock of hair she had set aside, the lass twisted several thin strands together to form strong, elegant strings for the harp. She stretched the strings tight and set them in tune, and when she plucked a note it was so full of longing and grief that even the birds winging their way to sea stopped to listen.

The lass set her white cloak around her shoulders, held the golden harp to her chest, and set out to the Sìdhean. As she traveled, villagers stepped aside for her to pass, according her the respect due a princess. But of this she noticed nothing. She walked the high road and the byroads, her eyes looking all about her for a secret gateway into the hollow hills.

At last, Rosemary found a narrow crack into a high mound of green grass, its way guarded by an ancient, gnarled thorn tree. The lass waited there for the sun to set and the moon to rise, her heart thudding in her chest.

Before long, one of the faery folk rode towards her. Tall and slender, with skin so white it gleamed in the twilight, her dark hair tumbled down her back. She was dressed in a glimmering gown woven from spider silk and thistledown, and rode on the back of a huge black horse that reared when it scented the lass hiding in the shadows, showing sharp white fangs in its red mouth.

The Sìdh turned her narrow, pointed face and looked directly at the lass as if she was not hidden in shadows. "How dare you lurk at my gateway," she said, her voice sweet and yet somehow cruel. "Those of human blood are not permitted here."

"I have brought you something wondrous fair," Rosemary replied, and stepped forward, swirling the cloak about her. "'Tis woven with my own bare hands, and embroidered with the gold of my own hair, and there is none like it anywhere else in the world."

A gleam of desire entered the Sìdh's slanted eyes. "With a cloak like that, I shall look like a queen," she whispered. "Give it to me!"

"There is a price," the lass replied, drawing the cloak close about her.

"There is always a price," the Sìdh answered with a sneer. "What is yours? Faery gold, I expect."

"I have no need of gold," the lass replied, hoping the cloak hid the trembling of her limbs. "No, all I wish is for you to take me inside the hollow hill, and down to the halls of the palace where the faery folk meet."

"What a fool," the Sìdh answered. "They shall never let you leave."

But the lass was adamant, so the faery shrugged and took her by the hand. Together, they entered through the narrow gateway guarded by the ancient thorn tree. Inside, all was darkness. The lass clung to the faery's cold hand. They seemed to walk for a very long time, and the lass felt icy winds blow upon her from other dark gaping holes and chasms. But she did not stumble, nor stub her bare toes on rocks, or bang her elbow against the walls. Nor did she shiver with cold, or tremble with fear. The lass was more grateful than ever that she was still protected by the old Gypsy's spell.

Faint music, spiraled up from somewhere far below. Down, down, down, the lass and the Sìdh walked, hand in hand. Soon the darkness was lit by tiny dancing flames, as white as starshine. The Sìdh preceded her onto a wide staircase made of the entwining branches of polished golden wood. It led down to a vast, dark hall where faeries of all shapes and sizes danced and laughed and feasted. Some were short and squat and hideous. Some were tall and pale and lovely. Some were as tiny as a sycamore seed. Others were as huge and rough pelted as a crag of rock. They all gazed in astonishment at the sight of the lass with her tangled hair and queenly white cloak.

"I have brought you within. Now give me the cloak!" The Sìdh snatched the soft white cloak from the lass's shoulders, and Rosemary let it go with a smile. Glancing back, she saw the Sìdh showing off the cloak and a crowd of other tall, dark faeries surrounding her, touching it, begging to be allowed to try it on.

Rosemary headed straight forward, harp in hand, until she spied a high throne at the far end of the cavernous hall. Like the staircase, it was made of entwining branches of some golden wood. Sitting upon it was a tall man with a frowning face and sharp-pointed ears. *He must be the new king of the Sìdh*, she thought.

Fearlessly, she approached the throne.

"You dare to approach the Elder Throne!" cried the king. "How did you – a human! – get inside the hollow hills?"

"I bring you something wondrous fair, my lord," Rosemary said, and she held out the harp. "'Tis made with my own bare hands and strung with my own golden hair and there's none like it anywhere else in the world."

"I have harps aplenty," shrugged the king.

"Not like this one," said the lass. She plucked a few chords, and the notes rang out so pure and transcendent that the king stared in wonder. His dark eyes lit with the flame of desire.

"You offer this as a gift for me, the new king of the Sìdhean?"

"There is a price," said the lass, holding the harp close to her.

"Of course there is," the king answered. He snapped his fingers and called, "Faery gold for the human."

A procession of Sìdh carried armfuls of gold and jewels from the treasure chamber and piled them high around Rosemary's bare ankles. "Surely," the king sneered, "that's more than enough payment for a common harp."

"I do not want gold," the lass said. "I do not want jewels. There is only one thing in this world that I want."

"Indeed?" The king arched an eyebrow. "What is that?"

"My bairn!" she cried. "He was stolen by the Sìdh after I left him in his blankets by the black cliffs. Give me back my bairn, and the harp is yours!"

The King of the Sìdhean frowned and shook his head. "The child is ours now. You know that we live long lives, but few children are born to us. We need young ones to keep our world from dying. You cannot have him back."

"He is mine!" Rosemary declared. "You had no right to take him."

"I am the King of the Sìdhean. I will do whatever I please," he answered.

"Then you will not have my harp!" She began to play a wild lament, so sad that all who listened felt tears burn their eyes. The king motioned to her to stop, but she defied him, her fingers flying over the golden strings spun from her own hair.

"I'll give you all the treasures of my kingdom," he cried, and clicked his fingers again. The Sìdh brought armfuls of diamonds and emeralds and rubies, worked in gleaming gold, and heaped them about her till she stood in jewels to her waist.

The lass kept on playing, however, and she sang in a voice that broke with tears:

"All I want is my own son,
for him I searched high and low,
for him I suffered such woe,
for him I have toiled and spun,
all I want is my own son."

The king was so moved by her song that his eyes grew wet. He covered his face with his hand and murmured, "Indeed, a harp that plays such a lament is worth more than the life of a human babe." He raised his fierce dark face. "Bring me the child!"

An old faery woman brought the baby forward. Although he was now swaddled in the finest silk, the lass knew his tuft of golden hair at once. "My bairn!" she cried.

At once the little boy recognized his mother's voice, and reached out. The lass took him in her arms, and let the harp fall. The old woman caught it and took it to the king, who at once began to play. All the Sìdh gathered around, moved beyond words by the beauty of the music.

Clutching her baby, the lass turned away from the king and went with swift, light steps up the curving staircase and through the dark passages till she reached the crack of light that would lead her back to the ordinary world. With every step, the sweet beguiling music grew fainter till at last – as the lass stepped out into a bright new dawn – she could hear it no longer.

She smiled and kissed her baby's soft cheek. "I have you back again," she whispered. "What fools they were to think a cloak of feathers and a harp of bone and hair were worth more than you!"

And she walked away, her bairn in her arms, back to the village of the kind fisherman who had saved her. And the Gypsies always knew they would be welcome at her home. Together they would feast and dance and sing, even if the tune was played on a flute carved from driftwood and not a magical harp with golden strings.

Kate says:

I first heard about this story when Lorena and I connected online. I had just finished my Doctorate of Creative Arts in fairy tale studies and wanted to buy myself a beautiful piece of fairy tale-inspired art to celebrate. A writer friend of mine tweeted about Lorena's work and I went to her website and discovered her beautiful, eerie artworks. I particularly loved her illustration of the mother making the magical harp and contacted Lorena, asking if I could buy it. It now hangs in my hallway, enchanting all who see it.

Chosen by Lorena, who says:

"The Stolen Bairn and the Sídh" is one of my favorite tales, and the first I illustrated for this book. On the surface, it could be read as a simple quest story, but within it is the powerful magic borne of a mother's love. The single mother takes on the hero's role and, with intelligence and bravery, is steadfast in her determination to find her child.

I first came across the story in Kathleen Ragan's *Fearless Girls, Wise Women & Beloved Sisters* and loved it immediately and completely, for its lack of fairy tale clichés, and for its focus on parental love. There are no knights in shining armor, no glass slippers or stolen kisses: just the "wild love and longing" of a mother for her child. With its strong focus on female independence, it is a fairy tale I'm very glad to pass onto my daughters.

"The Toy Princess" is the story of a princess born into a world that values the rigid etiquette of its court more than truthfulness and openness. Her fairy godmother replaces her with a toy princess who can only speak a few formulaic sentences so the girl can escape and find honest work and true love instead. It is a literary fairy tale written by the Pre-Raphaelite author Mary de Morgan and included in her first collection of stories, *On A Pincushion*, in 1877.

The Toy Princess

More than a thousand years ago, in a country quite on the other side of the world, people had grown so polite that they hardly ever spoke to each other.

They never said more than "Just so," "Yes indeed," "Thank you" and "If you please." And it was thought to be the rudest thing in the world for anyone to say they liked or disliked, or loved or hated, or were happy or miserable. No one ever laughed aloud, and if anyone had been seen to cry, they would have caused much embarrassment.

The king of this country married a princess from a neighboring land. The people in her home were as unlike her husband's people as it was possible to be. They laughed, and talked, and were merry when they were happy, and lamented if they were sad. In fact, whatever they felt they showed at once, and the princess was just like them.

When she came to her new home, she could not at all understand why everyone was so distant and formal. She pined for her own old home, growing thinner and paler every day. When she knew her end was drawing near, the queen sent for her faery godmother, Taboret, and had a long talk with her alone. No one knew what was said, but soon afterwards a little princess was born, and the queen died.

Of course, all the courtiers were sorry for the poor queen's death, but it would have been thought rude to say so. So, although there was a grand funeral, nobody wept and nobody sighed.

Nobody, except for the newborn baby, who had been christened Ursula. She cried very loudly indeed, and nothing could stop her. All her ladies-in-waiting said they had never heard such a dreadful noise. "Be quiet," they told her. "Sit still. Be good. Children should be seen and not heard."

It was not long before Ursula learned that she must be good and quiet at all times.

She was a pretty little girl, with a round face and merry blue eyes. But as she grew older, her eyes grew less merry and bright, and her face grew thin and pale. She was not allowed to play with any other children, lest she might learn bad manners; she was not taught any games or given any toys. Instead, she passed most of her time at her lessons, or looking out of the window at the birds flying against the sky.

One day the old faery Taboret flew over to the King's palace to see how things were with the young princess. She saw Ursula sitting by the window, her head leaning on her hand.

"Your Royal Highness's dinner is now ready," said her lady-in-waiting.

"I don't wish for anything," Ursula replied, without turning her head.

"I believe I have told your Royal Highness before that it is not polite to speak of what you want or don't want," said the lady-in-waiting. "We are waiting for your Royal Highness."

So the Princess did as she was told.

"Sit up straight," the lady-in-waiting said. "Take only a morsel of food at a time. Do not talk with your mouth full. Do not clatter your knife against your plate in such a noisy fashion. Now nod and smile and say thank you to me."

"Thank you," Ursula answered, trying hard not to forget anything she had been told.

When Taboret saw how pale Ursula was, and that there was no talking or laughing allowed, she frowned. She flew back to her own home, and spent a long while thinking of what could be done.

The next day she paid a visit to the largest toy shop in Faeryland. It was a vast place, with shelves from floor to ceiling lined with the most extraordinary collection of toys you can imagine. Tin soldiers who marched up and down, crying "Left! Right!" in high, tinny voices. A tiny lion that roared and shook its magnificent mane. A mechanical golden lark in a golden cage that sang the sweetest song. Rocking horses that could carry one for miles across the

fields. Dolls whose eyes lit up and talked. A nutcracker in the shape of a red-coated trooper with a sword by his side. A toy dog who barked and a toy cat who purred. A golden harp that played its own strings. A wooden train that raced past on wooden tracks, puffing black smoke and whistling. A hut on chicken legs that strutted about, cock-a-doodle-dooing.

Taboret was well known in the shop as a good customer, and the master of the shop came forward to meet her at once, bowing and begging to know what he could get for her.

"I want," said Taboret, "a princess."

"A princess!" said the shop man, who was really an old wizard. "What size do you want it? I have one or two in stock."

"It should look about six years old now, but must grow."

"I can make you one," said the wizard, "but it'll come rather expensive."

"I don't mind that," said Taboret. "See! I want it to look exactly like this," and so saying she took a portrait of Ursula out of her bosom and gave it to the old man, who examined it carefully.

"I'll get it for you," he said. "When will you want it?"

"As soon as possible," said Taboret. "By tomorrow evening if possible. How much will it cost?"

"It'll cost you a fortune," the wizard said. "A walking talking princess doll is not cheap to create."

"It need not be at all talkative," said Taboret, "so that won't add much to the price. It need only say, "If you please," "No, thank you," "Certainly" and "Just so.""

"Well, under those circumstances," said the wizard, "I will do it for four cats' footfalls, two fish's screams, and two swans' songs."

"It is too much," cried Taboret. "I'll give you the footfalls and the screams, but to ask for swans' songs!"

"I can't do it for less," said the wizard, "and if you think it too much, you'd better try another shop."

Taboret sighed. "As I am really in a hurry for it, and cannot spend time in searching about, I suppose I must have it, but I consider the price very high. When will it be ready?"

"By tomorrow evening."

"Very well, then. Whatever you do, don't make it at all noisy or rough in its ways," she said.

The next evening the wizard showed her a pretty little girl so like Princess Ursula that no one could have told them apart.

"Well," said Taboret, "it looks well enough. But are you sure that it's a good piece of workmanship, and won't give way anywhere?"

"It's as good a piece of work as ever was done," said the wizard, proudly. "There's not one faery in twenty who could tell it from the real thing, and no mortal could."

"It seems to be fairly made," said Taboret, as she turned the little girl around. "Now I'll pay you."

Raising her wand in the air, she waved it three times. A series of strange sounds arose. The first was a low tramping, the second shrill and piercing screams, the third voices of wonderful beauty singing a sorrowful song. The wizard caught all the sounds and pocketed them at once, while Taboret picked up the toy princess, tucked her under her arm, and flew away.

At court that night, the real princess was curled up on the window seat, looking wistfully at the moon. "I wonder if they let you laugh and play and dance up there, Moon so bright? If so, I'd like to go and live with you – I'm sure it would be nicer than being here."

"Would you like to go away with me?"

Looking up, Ursula saw an old woman in a red cloak. Though her nose was hooked and her chin long, the old woman had a kind smile and bright black eyes, and so Ursula was not frightened.

"Where would you take me?" said the little princess.

"I'd take you to the seashore, where you'd be able to play about on the sands, and where you'd have some little boys and girls to play with, and no one to tell you not to make a noise."

"I'll go," cried Ursula, springing up at once.

"Come along," said the old woman, taking her tenderly in her arms and folding her in her warm red cloak. They rose up in the air, and flew out the window, away over the spires of the castle and the steep rooftops of the town.

The night air was sharp, and Ursula soon fell asleep; but still they kept flying on, on, over hill and dale, for miles and miles, away from the palace, towards the sea.

Far away from the court and the palace, was a hut in a tiny fishing village where a fisherman named Mark lived with his wife and three children. He was a poor man, but they were happy. The children, Oliver, Philip, and little Bell, were rosy cheeked and bright eyed. They played all day long on the shore, and shouted till they were hoarse.

It was to this village the faery bore the still-sleeping Ursula, and gently placed her on the doorstep of Mark's cottage. The fisherman and his wife were sitting quietly within. She was making the children clothes, and he was mending his net, when without any noise the door opened and the cold night air blew in.

"Wife," said the fisherman, "see who's at the door."

The wife got up and went to the door, and there lay Ursula, still sleeping soundly, in her white nightdress.

"Why, it's a little girl!" The wife carried her into the cottage. When she was brought into the warmth and light, Ursula awoke, and stared about her in fright. She did not cry, as another child might have done, but she trembled very much, and was almost too frightened to speak.

"Who are you? Where do you come from?" the fisherman asked gently.

"I … I don't know. I don't remember," Ursula answered hesitantly. It felt strange to have no memory, and she looked about her in bewilderment.

"What is your name? Do you remember that?" Mark asked.

"Ursula," the child answered, pleased that she had not forgotten everything.

"Are you hungry?" the fisherman's wife asked, and Ursula nodded eagerly.

"It'd be cruel to make her leave on such a cold night," the fisherman's wife said to her husband in a low voice, as Ursula ate some bread and milk. "We will try and find her folks in the morning."

When the court ladies came to wake Princess Ursula, little did they think it was a toy princess placed there in her stead. Indeed, the ladies were much pleased; for when they said "It is time for your Royal Highness to arise," she only answered, "Certainly" and let herself be dressed without another word. As the time passed, and she scarcely ever spoke, all said the princess was vastly improved.

In the meantime, in the fisherman's cottage far away, the real Ursula grew tall and straight as an alder and merry and lighthearted as a bird. She learned to bake bread and sew on patches and turn cartwheels on the sand, and she was so happy she sang and laughed from sunup to sundown.

Her old life was like a dream she barely remembered. But sometimes the mother would take out the little embroidered nightgown and show it to her, and wonder whence she came, and to whom she belonged.

"I don't care who I belong to," said Ursula, "as long as they don't come and take me away."

Years passed. The king was now an old man, and the toy princess was thought to be the most ladylike of all the women at court. Every one admired her manners, though she never said anything but "If you please," "No, thank you," "Certainly" and "Just so."

Meanwhile, at the cottage, the real princess Ursula grew more womanly every day and the fisherman and his wife grew bent and gray. Most of the work was now done by their eldest son, Oliver, who was their great pride. Ursula waited on them, and cleaned the house, and did the needlework, and was so useful that they could not have done without her. The faery Taboret came to the cottage from time to time, unseen by anyone, and, always finding Ursula healthy and merry, was pleased to think of how she had saved her from a dreadful life.

But one evening when she paid them a visit, not having been there for some time, she saw something which made her reconsider. Oliver and Ursula were standing together watching the waves, hands entwined.

"When we are married," said Oliver, softly, "we will live in that little cottage yonder, so that we can come and see them every day. But that will not be till little Bell is old enough to take your place, for how would my mother do without you?"

"And we had better not tell them," said Ursula, "that we mean to marry, or else the thought that they are preventing us will make them unhappy."

Taboret's face became grave. She walked up and down for a long time, pondering what to do. At last she flew back to the royal court. She found the King in the middle of a state council. On seeing this, she at once made herself visible.

"You find us," said his Majesty, "just about to resign our scepter into younger and more vigorous hands. In fact, we think we are growing too old to reign, and mean to abdicate in favor of our dear daughter, who will reign in our stead."

"Before you do any such thing," said Taboret, "let me have a little private conversation with you." Much to his surprise, she led the King into a corner.

When he returned to the council, all the color had drained from his face.

"My lords," he faltered, "pray pardon this extraordinary behavior. We have just received a dreadful blow. We hear on authority, which we cannot doubt, that our dear, dear daughter—" sobs choked his voice, and he was almost unable to proceed, "—is … is … in fact, not our daughter at all. She is a toy princess. A sham." He sank back in his chair, overpowered with grief.

The faery Taboret stepped to the front, and told the courtiers the whole story –

how she had stolen the real princess, because she feared they were ruining her, and how she had placed a toy princess in her place. The courtiers looked from one to another in surprise, but it was evident they did not believe a word she said.

"The princess is a truly charming young lady," said the Prime Minister.

"Has your Majesty any reason to complain of her Royal Highness's conduct?" asked the old Chancellor.

"None whatever," sobbed the King, "she was ever an excellent daughter."

"Then I don't see," said the Chancellor, "what reason your Majesty can have for paying any attention to what this – this person says."

"If you don't believe me, you old idiots," cried Taboret, "call the Princess here, and I'll soon prove my words."

"By all means," they retorted.

The King commanded that her Royal Highness should be summoned. In a few minutes she came, attended by her ladies. She said nothing, but then she never did speak till she was spoken to. So she entered, and stood in the middle of the room silently.

Without any ceremony, Taboret advanced towards the toy princess, and struck her lightly on the head with her wand. The head rolled on the floor, leaving the toy's body standing motionless as before. All could see that she was but a metal shell, motored by all sorts of cogs and wheels and wires.

"Just so," said the head, as it rolled towards the king. He and the courtiers picked up their robes and scattered out of its way.

When they were a little recovered, the King spoke again. "The faery tells me," he said, "that there is somewhere a real princess whom she wishes us to adopt as our daughter. And in the meantime, let her Royal Highness be carefully placed in a cupboard, and a general mourning be proclaimed for this dire event."

He glanced tenderly at the toy princess's mechanical body, and turned weeping away.

That evening the faery flew to the fisherman's cottage, and told them the whole truth about Ursula.

"A princess? Our Ursula?" the fisherman said.

"I always wondered," the fisherman's wife said, clasping Ursula close. "That silken nightgown we found you in … I'd never seen the like."

"I suppose you must return to your own folk now," the fisherman said sadly.

"Don't go, don't go!" Bell burst into tears, while Oliver set his jaw and looked away. Poor Ursula sobbed bitterly.

"Never mind," she cried after a time, "if I am really a princess, I will have you all to live with me. I am sure the king, my father, will wish it, when he hears how good you have all been to me."

On the appointed day, Taboret came for Ursula in a coach and four, and drove her away to the court. She stopped on the way and had the Princess dressed in a splendid white silk dress trimmed with gold, and strung pearls round her neck and in her hair, that she might appear properly at court. The King and all the council were assembled with great pomp, to greet their new Princess, and all looked grave and anxious. At last the door opened, and Taboret appeared, leading the young woman by the hand.

"That is your father!" said she to Ursula, pointing to the King; and on this, Ursula, needing no other bidding, ran at once to him, and kissed him.

All the courtiers gasped with horror.

"This is really!" said one.

"This is truly!" said another.

"What have I done?" cried Ursula. "Have I kissed the wrong person?"

Everyone groaned.

"Come now," cried Taboret, "if you don't like her, I shall take her away to those who do. I'll give you a week, and then I'll come back and see how you're treating her. She's a great deal too good for any of you."

So saying, she flew away on her wand, leaving Ursula to get on with her new friends as best she might.

But it was no use. If she spoke or moved they looked shocked, and at last she was so frightened and troubled by them that she burst into tears, at which they were more shocked still.

"This is indeed a change after our sweet Princess," said one lady to another.

"Yes, indeed," was the answer, "when one remembers how even after her head was struck off she behaved so beautifully, and only said, 'Just so.'"

All the ladies disliked poor Ursula, and showed it. By the end of the week, she had grown quite thin and pale, and seemed afraid of speaking above a whisper.

"Why, what is wrong?" cried Taboret, when she returned. "Don't you like being here? Aren't they kind to you?"

"Take me back, dear Taboret," cried Ursula, weeping. "Take me back to Oliver and Philip, and Bell. As for these people, I hate them."

Taboret only smiled and patted her head, and then went into the king and courtiers.

"Now, how is it," she cried, "I find Princess Ursula in tears? When you had that metal-and-leather Princess, you could behave well enough to it, but now that you have a real flesh-and-blood woman, none of you care for her."

"Our late dear daughter—" began the King, when the faery interrupted him.

"I do believe," she said, "that you would like to have the doll back again. Now I will give you a choice. Which will you have – my Princess Ursula, the real one, or your Princess Ursula, the sham?"

The King sank back into his chair.

"I am not equal to this," he said. "Summon the council, and let them settle it by vote."

"Let both Princesses be fetched," the faery said.

The toy princess was brought from her cupboard, and stood quietly, her head in the crook of her arm, showing all the metal coils and cogs hanging loose. The real princess rushed in with her eyes red and swollen, her hair disheveled and her fine silk dress crushed.

"I should think there could be no doubt which one we would prefer," said the Prime Minister to the Chancellor.

"I should think not either," answered the Chancellor.

"Then vote," said Taboret.

Every vote was for the sham Ursula, and not one for the real one.

Taboret laughed. "You're a pack of sillies,
but you shall have what you want."

She picked up the head, and with a wave of her wand, stuck it onto the body.

The toy princess moved around slowly and said, "Certainly," in its old voice. On hearing this, all the courtiers gave something as close to a cheer as they thought polite.

"We will," the king cried, "at once make our arrangements for abdicating and leaving the government in the hands of our dear daughter."

Taboret laughed scornfully. Taking up the real Ursula in her arms, she flew back with her to the fisherman's cottage.

At the royal court, there were great rejoicings at the recovery of the princess, who bowed her smooth head and said, "Just so."

But Ursula ran barefoot and laughing along the beach, hand in hand with Oliver.

Chosen by Kate, who says:

I discovered the literary fairy tales of Mary de Morgan quite by accident, while researching William Morris and the Pre-Raphaelites for my doctorate in fairy tale studies. I bought an old second-hand copy of her fairy tales and fell in love with them. I think it's such a shame her work is not as widely celebrated as other literary fairy tale tellers such as Hans Christian Andersen and Oscar Wilde. "The Toy Princess" turns the conventional format of traditional tale upside down, by having a princess transformed into just an ordinary girl. She learns to laugh and cry and work for her living, and is far happier than she ever was in the stifled world of the royal court.

Lorena says:

I wasn't aware of "The Toy Princess" until Kate recommended we include it in this book. It took one read through the story for it to fill my mind with images. Especially the toy shop! If you look closely on the shelves, you'll find creatures and elements from the other stories in the book. Count them and let me know how many you find! Be warned though, there are some red herrings …

What I love about this tale, as Kate mentions above, is how the princess story is inverted. She leaves the physical and emotional prison of court life to find liberation in hard work and a simpler existence. How tragic it is that she is rejected by her father for her "perfect" automaton self, but how wonderful that she finds freedom and a family to truly love her for herself.

Illustrator notes

If you look closely you'll see that these illustrations are different from most. They were made from many separate photographs, montaged together to create each final image. Some of them contain over 70 individual photographs, and the illustration of the toy shop has hundreds! The young women you see in these pages are Kate's and Lorena's daughters, and the twigs, bones and leaves are all gathered from backyard and bushland. They were photographed against a backlight to create a silhouette, then digitally assembled and placed within multilayered photographic backgrounds. The human figures are made from themselves, while the wild creatures are built up from tiny fragments of the landscape.

Walk outside and look down at your feet. That leaf could be the curve of a horse's back; the broken stick an outstretched arm. You are surrounded every day by the scraps of nature. What new creature could you create?

About the Author

Kate Forsyth wrote her first novel at the age of seven, and has since sold more than a million copies around the world. Her books for adults include *Bitter Greens,* a retelling of Rapunzel which won the 2015 American Library Association Award for Best Historical Fiction and *The Wild Girl,* the story of the forbidden romance behind the Grimm Brothers' famous fairy tales, which was named the Most Memorable Love Story of 2013.

Kate's books for children include the collection of fairy tale retellings *Vasilisa the Wise & Other Tales of Brave Young Women,* illustrated by Lorena Carrington; *The Impossible Quest,* her five-book fantasy adventure series, which has been optioned for a film; and *The Puzzle Ring,* named an "Unsung Hero" of 2009 by international bloggers.

Kate has a BA in literature, a MA in creative writing and a Doctorate of Creative Arts in fairy tale studies. Her doctoral exegesis, "The Rebirth of Rapunzel: A Mythic History of the Maiden in the Tower," won the Aurealis Convenors' Award for Excellence in 2016 and the William Atheling Jr Award for Criticism in 2017. Kate is a direct descendant of Charlotte Waring Atkinson, the author of the first book for children ever published in Australia. An accredited master storyteller, Kate has taught and told stories all over the world.

Read more about her at her website.

About the Illustrator

Lorena Carrington is a photographic artist and illustrator with an interest in lost and forgotten fairy tales. She exhibits widely, has work in national and international collections, and also runs workshops in art, illustration and the relationship between text and image. She grew up in a library and art studio so, after working as a photographer and practicing artist for nearly twenty years, creating books feels like coming home.